OF SHADOWS AND ELVES

Of Goblin Kings Book 2

EMMA HAMM

If you read this
Tell the Goblin King
It was me...

(...who wrote the book. Do you know how hard these dedications are??
They can't always be serious.)

CHAPTER 1

They plotted rebellion over a cup of earl grey tea.

Three strange figures sat around a small wooden table in the middle of the underground home. A dog in a pressed velvet suit. A young man with the face of a rat and a tail that curled up behind him. And her sister, Esther, with her own fluffy white tail that wagged with frustration whenever one of the men spoke.

Freya stood in the doorway to the single bedroom, leaning against the doorframe, warming her fingers around the chipped, blue teacup in her hand.

It wasn't a particularly good cup of tea, if Freya was being honest. She blew on the top so it at least looked like she was drinking it. Poor Arrow would be insulted if she admitted that his prized talent of making tea wasn't a talent at all.

Her sister and the goblin boy were obviously feeling the same way. They looked at each other, then back to the mismatched porcelain as though the liquid might claw its way into their throats. The tea certainly had a bite to it.

Esther leaned forward, took her sixth cube of sugar, and plopped it into the cup. "So what you're saying is that the Goblin

Queen was the least favored candidate for the throne. That's why the King we know took it?"

"Yes," the goblin boy replied.

Lux, Freya reminded herself. He'd informed them that his name was Lux, and he'd appreciate it if Freya would stop referring to him as the rat goblin. Or the goblin boy. Or any of the other nicknames she'd come up with.

Her cheeks still burned at the memory. Old prejudices died hard, and she was trying her best. But sometimes that old hatred of the goblin kind spilled out of her mouth without her realizing just how horrible it sounded.

"If no one wanted her to lead all the faerie courts, then how did she take the throne?" Esther shook her head, clearly struggling with her thoughts. "We all know the Goblin King wanted Freya to defeat him. He practically handed her the victory on a golden platter."

"Excuse you," Freya interrupted. "If I hadn't had his help, I still would have beaten him."

"That's cute." Esther rolled her eyes. "He helped you far more than he should have if he knew he would lose the throne. Why would he be willing to give it up so easily if he had fought his entire life to keep it?"

Arrow stood and padded to the back of the room. He opened up the wall to reveal a pantry so stuffed with food that a couple tins jumped from a shelf and rolled across the floor.

He spoke while tossing random vegetables over his shoulder. "The King has strange ways. Perhaps he already knew the Goblin Queen was plotting against him again. At least losing the throne on his own terms means he has some kind of control."

Freya licked her lips. It didn't sound right, no matter how many times she rolled the theory over in her mind. "I don't think he'd give up that easily. And when I saw him last, it was almost as though he was in pain. Like he knew what was going to happen, and that he didn't want it to happen. But he still let it."

And that was the biggest question in her mind. The Goblin

King had made it so very clear that the only thing keeping him happy was that throne. He was proud to be the Goblin King. Everyone she'd spoken to actually liked him as their monarch. Even Arrow, who had lost his family in service to the fickle fae creature.

Pain bloomed behind her eyes, splitting between her brows and scissoring into her nose. The damned headache wouldn't go away, especially when she thought of the Goblin King.

She pinched the bridge of her nose and tried to blink through the pain.

"Cookie?" Arrow asked.

When she could open her eyes again, she peered down to see he had somehow pulled out a tray of tiny sugar cookies in the shape of stars. Maybe some sugar would do her headache good.

"Thank you," Freya muttered before popping one in her mouth and taking another. "Regardless, we need to know what will happen when the Queen is officially on the throne."

Arrow carried the silver tray to the table and set it down. "I think we already know that. The entire kingdom was crumbling around your ears when you ran away from that castle, Freya. She's only going to keep making it worse."

"And do we even know who she is?" That would make all this even more difficult if they didn't have the faintest idea of where to start.

Why did this feel as though she were back to the beginning of the story? Freya had fought through all four courts of the faeries to get her sister back, and she'd succeeded. Esther was sitting right there, within her reach. And yet somehow she was back to the start of yet another quest that would require her to search through places she hadn't the faintest idea how to navigate.

Arrow sat back down and held his snout in his hands.

Painful silence rang throughout the room. Freya looked between all three of them, guilty expressions painted across their faces.

"Well?" She asked again. "Out with it if you all know something I don't."

Lux cleared his throat. "The Goblin Queen is... well, sort of the Goblin King's sister."

He had a family? Freya hadn't ever given it much thought. She knew the other faeries did, of course. She'd seen the goblin children and their messy dinners. Obviously they had families somewhere that she hadn't met.

"Sister?" she asked. "What do you mean, *sort of* his sister?"

Esther frowned as well. "Why would his sister want to hurt him?"

Freya stepped up to the table and placed a hand on Esther's shoulder. They both were aware of what a sister would do to keep her sibling safe and unharmed. Even come all the way to the faerie realm and defeat a king.

"Well, he was born in the Autumn Court. Even became the Autumn Thief for a while there, but then some things happened and..." Lux ran a hand underneath the collar of his shirt. "He decided to go to the Winter Court, where things could cool off. They adopted him. And in the Faerie Wars, he fought by their side. So she wasn't really his sister by blood, but by circumstance. Anyway, after the war he became the Goblin King and sacrificed the entire Winter Court to save everyone else."

Freya remembered that bleak place and all the dead faeries who were forever frozen in time. "I saw them. They were terrifying and beautiful at the same time."

Arrow snuffled. "Sounds like the Winter Court. Regardless, they have a vendetta against the King for freezing them for an eternity. If she's out, that means the Goblin Queen will release all the Winter Court back to their rightful places. And they were known for their cruelty. In fact, I'd argue they were worse than any other court."

"Worse than the Spring Maiden?" Obviously Freya had her own thoughts on the matter. The Spring Maiden's court was by far the most alarming.

"Much worse." Arrow looked troubled by the thought, but he still stated his opinion firmly. "Perhaps we should enlist some of the other courts to help our plan."

"No," Lux replied. "We've been over this. The Goblin King is our problem, and any other courts getting involved would only make this an all out war."

"Maybe that's what everyone needs to see. The Goblin Queen is everyone's problem, not just the Autumn Court's."

"And you want to be one of the warriors in this upcoming war? A small dog with a penchant for suits?" Lux tossed his hands in the air, leaned forward, and the argument was back on.

They had talked about this for days since they arrived in Arrow's small home. Freya had heard every angle of their arguments at least twice.

Arrow didn't want to go into a battle without assistance. He believed the other courts would help them, and that it was smarter to have more allies when dealing with someone as powerful as the Goblin Queen.

Lux wanted to sneak into the castle without anyone knowing. He didn't want the Queen to realize what was happening, and he certainly didn't want the other courts involved. In his opinion, the only court that was worth its salt was the Goblin Court. Everyone else could no longer be trusted.

They would argue until they were blue in the face, but Freya already knew their opinions wouldn't change.

She squeezed Esther's shoulder, then knelt down beside her. "What do you think?"

Esther's eyes widened in surprise. "Well, I don't know. I'm not one to know what to do in a war."

"I don't think it has to be a war." She watched as Arrow stood up on his chair so he was at least the same height as Lux while he yelled. "I think if we get the Goblin King back, then he can take the throne from this woman. Obviously he did it before, and if we give him the tools to do so again..."

"Then he would." Esther nodded. "But how are we going to get him back is the question?"

"I'm afraid my imagination isn't that creative. What do you think?" Freya already knew her sister was smart, but now that Esther had been here for a while, Freya had to assume that her sister knew these people better. "You've lived with the goblins and met more fae than me. Surely you have some opinion?"

Maybe it was the first time she'd asked her sister for something so important. Or perhaps Esther was so used to being the child that she hadn't thought Freya would ask for her help.

Either way, Esther opened her mouth a couple times before she finally spat out words. "Uh, well, I think you should go alone. Or with a single guide. The Goblin Queen must be similar to the other fae we've met. Shiny, new things will keep her entertained while you search for the king. And you were the one who defeated him in the first place and put her on the throne. Why wouldn't you seek out this new queen for her favor? Considering you were the one to put her there."

It was the best plan Freya had heard yet.

Sure, there were a lot of holes in it. She could fail at any point, and most of the concept was making it up as she went along. But it was far better than reaching out to the other courts, and a hell of a lot better than some assassination mission.

Freya wasn't a killer. She didn't even know what she'd do with a sword.

She stood up and pressed her hand to the muscles of her aching back. "Enough, boys."

They continued to argue as though she hadn't said a word.

Anger flashed like lightning in her chest and this time, she shouted. "I said, enough!"

They both fell silent. Lux's cheeks burned bright red, and he sheepishly looked at her sister, then back at Freya. "My apologies, Freya. I got wrapped up in the argument, I suppose."

Arrow, on the other hand, didn't look like he was upset at all. He crossed his paws over his chest and stared at the other goblin with curled lips. "I'm not apologizing. This fool seems to think we're all warriors here. He needs to realize we're nothing more than a dandy dog, two mortal women, and a goblin who is barely more than a baby."

Lux lunged to his feet and pointed at the dog. "I've done more in my life—"

"What did I just say?" Freya snarled. The anger in her tone must have frightened both of them this time. Lux sat back down and Arrow stared at her with wide eyes.

She didn't want to argue with either of them. And she didn't want to scold them like they were children. But they both needed to listen to her without trying to put their own opinions on the table.

"As far as I see it, this downfall of the courts is my fault." Freya lifted her hand for silence when Arrow opened his mouth. "No, listen to me. This is my fault because I was the one who beat him. No one else had ever done so, regardless if he helped. I still was the one to beat him. I was the one to put the Goblin Queen on that throne."

It was hard to admit. The truth sometimes stung, and she needed to figure out how to fix this. If they couldn't ask the other courts, and they couldn't work together, then she would just do it herself.

Freya was used to that, anyway. She almost preferred working on her own.

"So," she continued. "I think I'm going to make a plea to the Goblin Queen."

"Excuse me?" Arrow replied. "You will do no such thing. She's a mad woman!"

"For once, I agree with the dog." Lux leaned back and crossed his arms over his chest. "The Goblin Queen isn't someone you can defeat in a battle of wits. If you thought the Goblin King was difficult, she's ten times worse."

"Then I will figure it out just as I did the Goblin King." Freya shrugged. "This isn't up for debate, gentlemen. I've listened to the two of you argue every single day for the past week, and we've gotten nowhere. I'm the one who gave her the opportunity to take the throne, so she will be more likely to trust me. Don't you think?"

She put her hand on Esther's shoulder and smiled down at her little sister.

Esther nodded in agreement. "I believe this is the best choice for Freya. She'll sneak into the castle. Find the Goblin King. And then we can move on from there. The Queen won't stop her if she thinks that Freya hates the Goblin King just as much as she does."

Arrow curled his lips in a snarl once again. "And just who do you think is going to bring you to the Winter Court?"

"You, actually." Freya turned her grin on the dog. "You know the courts better than anyone else here. So I need you to bring me into the castle, and then you'll be my trusted advisor. An explanation for why I remained when I could have taken Esther and run."

"I think it's an awful plan."

Freya shrugged. "You think every plan is awful, Arrow. Now, why don't we prepare for a new adventure?"

CHAPTER 2

She let the boys continue arguing until they were blue in the face. Arrow and Lux were bound and determined to be the most knowledgeable about their own kind. And while she appreciated the help, most of the time she just wanted a straight answer.

Freya ducked into the single bedroom to gather her things. Not that she had a lot, but she had collected a few items she wanted to keep close to her person.

But in planning to leave, she realized that she would miss this earthen bound home. The dirt walls might have been off-putting to some. She found them cozy, even the little roots hanging from the ceiling. There was a single bunk bed in the corner, too small for either her or Lux to sleep on. So the two of them had laid blankets on the floor. The quilted, patchwork patterns were now dear to her.

These people had become her new family in such a short amount of time. Even the two goblins who she had once hated and feared.

Shaking her head, she tucked as many of her items into a leather bag. First, what little clothing she'd taken from her sister and a few others who had stopped by to visit. Then her boots, because she'd steal Esther's for walking to the castle. And lastly, the three items that the Goblin King had sent her to get.

She sat on the edge of the bunk where her sister slept and held the three pieces in her hands. A tiny little vial with a sprig of lavender. A little pot of perfume that had made her head spin and her mind forget everything. Lastly, the rolled up portrait of the Goblin King and herself.

How strange it was to think that she'd gathered these items only a few weeks ago when it felt like a lifetime. A battle between herself and the Goblin King should have taken years. They'd packed it into a few months.

Carefully, Freya unrolled the portrait and stared down into the Goblin King's eyes. He watched her with a severe expression befitting a king, but she thought maybe the portrait looked like he was furrowing his brows. In pain?

She leaned closer to look, only for that splitting headache to slice through her skull again. She hissed out a breath and touched her hand to her forehead, letting the portrait roll closed again.

"Freya?" Esther's voice broke through the pain. "Are you all right?"

No, she wasn't all right. This damned headache refused to go away, and it made it so difficult to focus. She could hardly breathe right now, and the pain was only getting more frequent. It seemed like it was coming back daily now.

But she couldn't tell her sister any of that. Not when she was planning to leave again.

Freya shook off the pain, opened her eyes, and smiled through gritted teeth. "Just a headache is all. I think it's from those nitwits yelling in the kitchen since we've gotten here. My ears are constantly ringing."

"The kitchen?" Esther grinned. "I would have called it the dining room."

"Perhaps the living area?"

The sound of her sister's giggle banished any lingering pain.

It was so good to hear Esther happy again. Had she laughed since they had lost their parents? Not like that.

Freya reached out her hands for Esther to take and drew her sister to sit beside her. "Thank you for helping in there. I don't think we'd have settled on any plan if the two of us hadn't thought of something."

"Neither of them are thrilled with this plan of ours."

"I didn't think they would be. But I also won't ask for their permission to fix something I broke." The headache bloomed again, and she winced. "I think I need some fresh air, regardless. That's what mother always did for her headaches."

Freya had completely forgotten about their mother's headaches until this moment. She'd always pressed her fingers to the same place, right in the center of her forehead, as though someone had struck her with a hammer.

How odd.

But she didn't have time to ponder what that meant. She had to pack and prepare herself for another journey, when she didn't know how far that journey was going to be. And she had to say goodbye to her dear sister, yet again.

Although, leaving her sister was easier this time. Esther didn't seem like the same little girl she remembered in their cottage. Something in this realm had changed her. Or maybe Freya was just seeing her for the adult she was and likely had been for a while now.

Esther reached for her hands and squeezed them tight. "I want to go with you."

The words hung between them, too dangerous to give proper thought. Esther couldn't come with Freya. Two mortal women wandering through the faerie realm would be foolish. The Goblin Queen would catch them, or some other faerie who wanted to entertain themselves with a human novelty. Not to mention Freya wouldn't be able to focus when she was trying to make sure her baby sister was safe.

"I don't think that's a good idea," she replied.

"Of course it is! We worked well together in the kitchen, and I think we could do that again. The sisters of Woolwich can defeat any faerie who walks before them." Esther squeezed her fingers again. "And I've missed you, even though I also feared what your thick skull would say when you found me."

She should have guessed Esther would say something like that. Sighing, Freya shook her head again. "I don't think the queen will want to see you, Esther. This entire plan is based on the fact that I saved you from the Goblin King, and then I stayed behind. Maybe that's part of the deal with the king, I don't know. I'm going to have to lie through my teeth and you'd be a distraction I can't afford."

Esther frowned, and the expression was one Freya knew well. Her little sister was about to explode with anger, and this little hovel might cave in under the power of her emotion. Esther knew how to shout so loud even the clouds hid from her rage.

But Lux moved into the doorway and cleared his throat. Esther's anger faded as she turned to look at the goblin boy she so clearly loved.

"Arrow has gone out to gather a few things for this new journey," he said. "But I agree with Freya. I think you should stay here with me."

"Why?" Esther asked. "Why should I stay here when there's so much for me to do? I could help her, Lux. You know as well as I that there's so much I could do here in the faerie realms."

"I do know that." He crossed his arms over his chest and his tail snapped with frustration. "I also know there's a lot of people who will need our help here, and I can't manage all on my own. The faerie courts are crumbling as we speak. Faeries from every season need someone to go to, and we're going to be the ones who guide them."

Freya thought that was a rather splendid idea. She met Lux's gaze and watched as he flicked his eyes to Esther, then back to Freya.

Right, she was supposed to help convince her sister.

Leaping into action, she released Esther's hands and got to her feet. "How many people will be affected by this?"

Lux took her cue and ran with it. He stepped into the room and waved his hands above his head. "Countless. Really, every court is going to need someone to guide them through this. The Goblin Queen doesn't care who she hurts as she forces her way onto the throne she's wanted for so long. We need to gather a haven for everyone."

"An army?" Freya couldn't help but poke at the argument he'd just been having.

His brows drew down tight and his jaw jumped. "No," he replied. "Not an army. This will be a refugee camp for those who want nothing to do with the queen. A place for like-minded individuals to find others who want to help."

"Right," Freya replied. She nodded and pursed her lips. "Of course, not an army. However, if I needed you to get involved when I end up in the Goblin Queen's new castle?"

"Freya," he snarled.

Esther stood from the bed with a sigh. "Stop arguing, you two. I can't take everyone being like this. I get what you're both bashing me in the skull with. You don't want me to go with Freya. Neither of you want me to, and apparently my opinion means nothing."

The last thing she wanted was for her sister to feel as though she was unwanted. Freya had just found Esther after tearing the world apart for her, and she craved time with her wayward sibling who always sought adventure.

In a way, Freya supposed that might bother Esther as well. Freya had never been the adventurous one. Esther was more likely to wander into the woods or plunge into a frigid lake to swim. Yet it was Freya who was having all the adventures here. Not the adventurous one.

She stepped close to her sister and cupped Esther's jaw. "If I could take you with me, you know I would. You've proven yourself quite useful, Esther. I couldn't have a more formidable partner if I searched all the corners of the earth."

"Then why aren't you taking me?"

"I need you to be here. With Lux. There are so many people who need help right now, and you two are the only ones who know how to get them to safety." Freya knew the excuse sounded flimsy at best, but it was the truth.

If there were people who needed help, then she would not stand by and let them flounder. Freya was responsible for their losses too. Someday, she hoped, she might be able to make it up to all the faeries who missed their king.

The padding footsteps of a small dog approached them through the earthbound home, and Arrow stuck his face around Lux's leg. "If we're going to the Winter Court, I assumed we would leave right now."

Freya supposed there was no time like the present. They'd already decided on the plan which wasn't much of one. They didn't have to argue about anything now.

Sighing, she reached for the bag she'd left on the bed. "A week off from adventure was rather nice, wouldn't you say?"

Arrow snorted. "You wouldn't know how to live a life without adventure if you tried."

She looked over at Esther, who had covered her mouth to hide her smile. If only the goblins knew just how unadventurous Freya really was. She wished she could play her life back for them in a dream bubble like in the Spring Court. They'd be shocked to see how little she had done in the mortal realm, and how much she had changed in a very short amount of time.

Grinning, she reached for her sister and drew Esther into her arms. "I'm going to miss you so much," she whispered into Esther's hair. "At least this time I get to say goodbye."

"I'm going to miss you too." Esther pressed her face into Freya's shoulder and for a second, it felt like nothing had changed at all.

They were still two sisters who had gone through hell

together. They had been raised to be strong and capable, but leaned on each other when they needed to. Even though everything had changed.

Esther wanted to stay here forever. She had a life with this goblin boy who had stolen her heart. And Freya?

Freya still had no one but herself and the hope that she could fix what she'd broken. What would happen after she did that? Where would she go once she'd pieced back together the shards of the faerie realm?

Sighing, she drew back and gave her sister a watery smile. "I'll be back before you know it. Just keep everyone safe while I'm gone."

Arrow's wet nose pressed against the back of her hand. "Excuse me. I don't care who's safe, I just want to make sure my house isn't ruined when I get back. Keep everything clean, Esther. Don't let anyone into the structure who's larger than Lux, for all the faerie realms. They'll tear the whole thing down by the roots and then where will I live?"

Leave it to Arrow to bring them all back to earth.

Freya rolled her eyes, stared up at the roots in the ceiling, then blew out a long, measured breath. "All right, Arrow. How are you getting us into the Winter Court?"

CHAPTER 3

Arrow had created a portal for them in the middle of his garden. Though it had no frame, the colorless surface looked eerily like a mirror. She stared into her reflection that was slightly off, perhaps a little more transparent than she would have expected. Almost as though the portal were made entirely out of ice.

"Ready?" she asked one last time.

"You know, if you keep asking that question, it will not make either of us more prepared." Arrow shuddered. "Just make sure your coat is buttoned all the way up. We're both going to be freezing the moment we step through that portal."

Right. Arrow had insisted she put on multiple layers of clothing, because apparently the last time she'd been in the Winter Court was enough to convince him that she didn't know how to be in snow.

She did. It snowed in Woolwich every year, and she'd always been fine. He still wouldn't listen to the truth that she hadn't exactly had the ability to pack jackets when she was racing to get her sister back before the time ran out.

Huffing out an angry breath, she tugged her hat lower over

her ears and fiddled with the mittens covering her hands. "Yes, I realize it's going to be cold."

He looked over at her with a calculating gaze, then nodded. "You look like a ball of yarn someone mangled."

"Thank you?" Though the words were a question. She watched as he stepped through the portal and disappeared.

The dog was a brat. Freya unfortunately didn't have time to scold the little rascal before he'd stepped through the portal. She supposed there was only one way to admonish him now, and that was to follow him into the depths of the Winter Court.

She didn't want to go back there.

Freya stepped through the portal herself and tried very hard not to wince at the feeling of ice shards sliding along her skin. Every portal was different, it seemed. This one was not friendly at all.

The cold pierced her skin in tiny daggers all over her body. It didn't matter that she was wearing warm clothing. The cold sliced through every woolen garment with ease. Icy wind dug into her flesh and poked at her very heart, stealing her breath away.

And stepping out onto the other side of the portal was no better. The very air filled her lungs with more ice shards and the cold stung her cheeks, reaching deep into the bones of her skull. Even her eyes felt like they were freezing in place.

Teeth chattering, she searched for Arrow. He had somehow pulled a hat out of his backpack and tugged it down over his very large ears. A small jacket covered his body from head to toe, but he still shivered uncontrollably.

"Is it colder than the last time I was here?" she asked, rubbing her arms. She thought she'd been able to stand in this barren wasteland in just a ball gown while she followed the hot springs. Now, as she searched for the warm rivers, there wasn't a steaming pool of water in sight. She feared even they might have frozen over.

The entire landscape before them was buried in snow. Drifts

of fluffy white ice buried anything that might have once been fences or gates. A few humps in the distance might hide houses, but she wasn't sure anymore. They might have also been giant creatures who had simply fallen where they stood.

Arrow huffed out a little angry breath. "I hate the Winter Court. This is why I didn't want to come with you last time."

The air between them turned even colder, if that was possible. They still hadn't talked about what had happened in the Autumn Court. Of course, she'd apologized, but he didn't wish to speak of the things that were said.

He'd still betrayed her. He'd gone behind her back and worked for his king, when she'd thought he was helping her. And worse, she had made it seem as though they would never be friends again.

Ignoring the conversation they needed to have was turning both of their stomachs. It made times like these with him, when they were both alone and capable of talking about what had happened, turn rapidly tense. The silence between them was filled with the anger of lies and heartbreak.

Was now the time to talk about it? Likely not. But she wanted to heal what had been broken.

Apparently that was a theme in her life these days.

"Arrow," she started, wondering how she was going to say the words that made her heart hurt. "I just wanted to say—"

"We have to keep moving," he interrupted. Arrow trotted through a snow drift, leaping into the air to get farther away from her with every bound. "We'll freeze in place if we don't. There should be a village up ahead where we can rest for the evening."

"Rest?" Freya trudged through the snow after him. "Why would we rest? Shouldn't we find the castle where the Goblin Queen is?"

"She'll find us," he muttered. "Don't you worry about that. No one comes into the Winter Court without her knowing."

Ominous. Freya didn't want to think about what the Goblin

Queen would send after them. The Spring Maiden's guards had been terrifying enough, and those were creatures who lived in the season when everything was coming to life. She imagined the Winter Court had frozen ghouls sent after people the Goblin Queen wanted to disappear.

Shivering uncontrollably now, she forced her way through the snow drifts and tucked her hands underneath her armpits. Keeping warm was the only thing she could think about right now, and that took all of her attention. She needed to focus on not shivering so hard that she'd fall onto her knees.

But damn, it was cold. The icy wind stole all sense and reason with every blow. She staggered through the snow and storm, but found it hard to take a step forward sometimes. Freya's mind wandered until she lost sight of Arrow as he bounded through the snow. Only to find him again when he picked up his head.

With the guidance of her trusty goblin dog, they made it to the village. Arrow stood at the top of a snow drift and waited for her to reach his side.

Lungs heaving, she stood beside him and eyed the abandoned place that wasn't yet buried in snow. There were ten houses all together, each with glass paned windows and roofs that were once thatched. Now, snow covered everything and barred the doors from anyone entering.

Or leaving.

Freya lifted her hands to her mouth and blew into them. "Where are all the people?"

"Gone," Arrow replied. "Does it really matter where they went?"

When they could be standing in the middle of a graveyard, yes, it mattered where they went. She wanted to know if these people had left of their own accord, or if some terrifying snow monster had removed them.

"Which house are we going into?" she asked.

"Pick one. I don't think there's anyone here."

She chose a house in the middle of the village. It felt safer to be hidden rather than on the end where any monster could appear out of the snow.

Freya put her mitten covered hands on the metal door knob and pulled hard. It took her ten yanks before the snow finally gave way and allowed enough space for Arrow and her to squeeze through. Once inside, she closed the door with a firm jerk, then locked it.

"You picked a decent one," Arrow said. "Now get a fire going before the two of us freeze solid."

She turned around and took in the interior. It had seen better days, but at least it wasn't dusty or cobweb ridden. Apparently the cold made even bugs disappear.

They stood in what she had to assume was the living area. Four doors on either wall likely led into the kitchen or bedroom. A large area rug covered the floor, woven by careful hands in what might have once been a bright red. Two rocking chairs sat in front of a stone fireplace with patchwork quilts over the backs. Curtains covered the windows in a color that must have once matched the rug.

"Cozy," she said as she approached the fireplace.

There were still logs ready to be lit. Like the first castle in the Winter Court, she had a feeling these were spelled so they would light easily and set off heat. Anyone who lived in a place like this would have to make sure such magic was available.

Bright flames burst into life the moment she touched a match to the wood. Heat spilled into the living area and the light gave everything a little more life. She tugged off her mittens and placed her hands before the heat.

"If we're resting for the night, I thought we could at least talk." Freya glanced over her shoulder and sighed.

One of the doors was ajar and there was no talking dog in sight.

"Fine," she whispered. "I guess it's just me for the night, then."

Freya sat down in one of the rocking chairs and set it into

motion. She stared into the flames, although she didn't feel all that tired. This adventure was vastly different from the last. She wasn't fighting for her sister's freedom, she was just trying to make up for the mistakes she'd made. And though she certainly was apologetic, part of this still felt like she was being punished for doing what she was supposed to do.

Beat the Goblin King.

That was her task, and she'd done it so well that the entire kingdom had fallen into shambles.

Maybe she should feel a little bad for it, but she didn't. Not really.

That headache bloomed behind her eyes again. This time it was far more painful than normal. It blistered through her skull and would have sent her to her knees if she hadn't been sitting down. The only thing that helped was staring into the fireplace, although that made no sense. Light should have made her headache worse.

She didn't know how long she remained still and quiet, but eventually she became aware that the other chair was moving. A shadow sat in it, or at least the shape of a man, and when she glanced over, her heart leapt in her chest.

The Goblin King sat beside her. He rested his hands on the chair arms, with clawed fingers dangling over the ends. The tufts of his ears were a little bare, and his skin was duller than she remembered. Even his clothing wasn't quite right. The normal crushed velvet black suit was gone, replaced only by a white shirt with an open collar, and black pants that were rather old. His feet were bare, toes curled on the floor as though he was cold. But he was here.

Impossibly.

She blinked a few times to clear her vision, but the Goblin King never disappeared. He really was sitting in the chair beside her, gently rocking and keeping pace with her movements.

"You can't be here," she whispered.

"Freya, haven't I proven to you enough times that impossible things are possible in the faerie realms?"

She gazed into those swirling silver eyes, and she knew it could be no one but him.

The Goblin King had somehow found her.

"I thought you were in a prison or wherever the Goblin Queen puts people she doesn't like." Freya stopped her rocking and noted he did the same. "We had our last conversation, and then the Goblin Queen took over. So you can't really be here."

"And yet, I am." He turned, and she noted how sunken his features were now. Almost as though he hadn't eaten in a very long time. "What are you doing here, Freya? You beat me. You can go home to your little cottage by the forest."

"My sister didn't want to go home. She wanted to stay here with that rat-faced goblin boy." Freya's stomach still twisted at the thought. "She's in love with him, or so she claims."

"Do you think it strange that a human and a goblin could fall in love?" There was a darkness in his eyes she wasn't used to. A serious nature that went against all he was.

Freya leaned forward and met his gaze without hesitation. "Are you all right?"

"Why do you ask?"

"You look..." She gestured up and down his body. "You don't look like yourself."

"Where do you think I am, Freya? In a prison, placed there by the Goblin Queen. I'm sorry I don't meet your fashion standards." He chuckled though, and the sound softened the bite of his words. "Now you haven't answered my question. Why are you still here?"

She didn't want to answer honestly. He'd take it personally and then run with it. She'd never hear the end of why she was here, and yet, she still had to tell him.

Freya leaned back in her chair and stared into the fire, because she refused to look at him while she said it. "I wronged you, Goblin King. I don't know if I would have changed my choices had I known defeating you meant throwing the faerie courts into a spiral. But I do know I would have figured out a different way. This is me fixing what I broke."

"Oh, Freya." The warmth in his voice had her turning to see a smile on his face. "Does that mean you like me after all?"

"Don't take this personally, Goblin King. I have a sense of honor. This doesn't mean I enjoy your company."

"I think it does." He grinned, but then started coughing.

The hacking sound echoed through the room. It was a horrible, lung deep sound that wasn't healthy. She'd only heard such a noise once, and the person hadn't lived through the night.

Freya leaned forward again, hand outstretched as though she might touch him. But at the last second, she thought better of it.

"Do you want a glass of water?" she asked. "Or is there anything else I can get you?"

"I'm not really here." He shrugged. "I suppose a glass of water wouldn't do anything at all, in the long run. It might make me more comfortable here, but not where I actually am."

"Where are you, then?" If she knew, then this would all be so much easier. She could go directly to where he was and save him.

The Goblin King chuckled. "Freya, you know that's not how any of this works. I can't tell you where I am."

"Can you at least tell me if you're safe?"

The shadows in his eyes darkened. His cheeks seemed to hollow even more, though she couldn't tell if that was the flickering of the light.

"No," he replied.

"No, as in you can't tell me? Or no, as in you aren't safe where you are?" Her heart thundered in her chest.

His answer was so important. He had to know her desire to know he was safe, even if they hadn't gotten along very well in her past adventure.

The Goblin King and her shared a strange bond. They were tied together because he'd freed her soul from a life of boredom and she had... Well, all of this was her fault.

Freya supposed he should hate her for that.

He never responded to her question. Instead, he stared into the fire.

She nodded, resolving not to push him when he was obviously affected by his location. "All right, then. I suppose we can just sit in silence then."

And they did. When she woke the next morning with a nasty crick in her neck, it was as if the Goblin King had never been here at all. Except for the faint smell of apple pie that still lingered in the air.

CHAPTER 4

Arrow wiggled his way back into his jacket and sighed. "I don't want to go back out there," he grumbled. "It's too cold."

She also didn't want to dive back into the snow. But the morning came with a bright sun and glistening diamond chips on top of the ground outside the windows. They didn't have time to waste, and obviously the queen wasn't going to find them today.

So they had to continue on. Otherwise, they would get nowhere and the Goblin King would remain in his prison.

"I know," she replied. She shrugged into her own coat with a sad sigh. "I don't want to go out there either. But we don't have a choice, do we?"

"I suppose we don't. Since you dragged me all the way here."

Dragged? That was the game he was going to play? Arrow would pretend that she had forced him to come here, even though he'd volunteered himself for the difficult task.

Lux would have come in a heartbeat. The goblin boy had more in him than most, and he wanted to prove his bravery to any and everyone. Hell, he probably wanted to prove himself to the Goblin King and earn a favor.

She didn't know what Lux's plan was, neither did he, but she knew for a fact that he would have jumped if Freya asked him to come.

What she didn't know was why Arrow wanted to help after all that had happened between them. If he was going to be so awkward through the ordeal, why not just send the younger goblin and be done with it?

If only he would listen to her for a few minutes and let her ask.

Freya put her shoulder to the door, shoved the snow out of the way, and then gestured for Arrow to follow her. "Come on, then. Let's get this over with."

Arrow trotted out into the snow and put his nose up in the air. "There's a strange scent in the cabin this morning. Did you notice it?"

She stepped out into the fresh smell and nodded. "Yes, the Goblin King came to visit last night."

Arrow froze ahead of her. He lifted one back foot up, curling his toes against the cold, and then stammered, "Pardon me?"

"Well, I don't think it was really him," she clarified. Freya crunched through the snow and winced as she broke through the frozen top. "Maybe the right way to say it is that I saw a projection of him. He appeared last night when I was sitting before the fire. He... he didn't look like himself."

"No, I imagine he didn't." Arrow stared off into the distance, then started moving forward again. "The Goblin Queen was not kind to him, even when he lived with her all those years ago. At least, that's what my father always said. I was just a young goblin at the time, but I remember her."

Freya followed him over the ice and snow drifts, hoping that he'd continue the story in as much detail as possible. She found herself curious about the life the Goblin King had led.

"I probably shouldn't call him the Goblin King anymore, should I?" she muttered. "He's not the King. He's not the Autumn Thief either."

"He's just Eldridge now." Arrow kicked snow behind him in

an angry gesture. "It seems wrong. He's so much more than that."

"I suppose." The sun beating down on her back at least gave off some semblance of heat. That warmth would make today's journey a little easier. "So what do you think the Goblin Queen's plans are?"

"She'll make an example of him. Eldridge will become a symbol of all the people who rose up against her, and all the people she denied peace or happiness." He frowned, clearly disturbed by the thought. "She was always a twisted creature. She'd rather harm than heal."

Freya followed his winding path, feeling as though she was lucky to actually have a guide this time. At the very least, Arrow pretended like he knew where they were going and that meant the world to her.

But when the silence between them drew too thin, she knew she had to ask more things about the Goblin Queen, or let all the poisonous guilt in her chest fly free. And considering the way his hackles rose whenever she started to speak, Freya thought it likely that Arrow wasn't quite ready to talk yet.

So this time, when she took a deep breath to talk, she asked another question. "What do you mean that the Goblin Queen was always a twisted creature?"

He jumped at the opportunity to explain himself and not talk about the apologies still left unsaid between them. "Even when she wasn't this version of herself, back when they took Eldridge into their family, she liked pain. I remember how the servants said she would kick them if they did something she didn't like. Little things like that. Everyone knew to stay out of her way."

"She sounds like a lovely person," she said sarcastically. "I still don't understand why she'd want to hurt the Goblin King, however."

"Well, he was her brother. And if we were crowning people based on power, she was the logical choice for Goblin Queen. But no one wanted her on the throne. We all knew what would happen if she was given that kind of power." A shiver of dread shook through his body. "No good would come from that. We all knew and none of us wanted to take that risk."

She pushed through a snowdrift that was as tall as her waist and pondered on his words.

The Goblin King had been close to this woman. And she still couldn't even think of the Goblin King by his first name. It seemed like something he should give her, or at least permit her to use. Even in her own thoughts.

She leaned down and picked Arrow up as he struggled to get through the snow. Holding the goblin underneath her arm, she continued forward as though nothing odd was happening. "The Goblin King and her must never have had a very good relationship then."

"One would think they should feel nothing but disdain," Arrow replied, wiggling his legs to be put down. "But they were rather fond of each other if the rumors are true."

Why did that make her stomach churn in her belly? Even her heart skipped a beat at the thought.

There was no reason for her to be jealous of a cruel woman. The Goblin King wouldn't fall under the spell of a wicked creature like that. For all he was a fickle creature, he had a pure spirit, and he didn't like other people being harmed. Especially his own people.

Shaking her head, she forced the thoughts out of her mind. "And now?" She had to ask the question. She had to know if they were still close.

Arrow still struggled to be free of her arms. "I assume they hate each other now. Put me down, Freya."

She placed the goblin down onto the ground and tried to calm the rolling thoughts in her mind. She needed to focus on the here and now. They were still fighting a very real threat of freezing to death. She couldn't forget the quest at hand just because she'd found out something she didn't want to hear.

Freya put a hand to her head and sighed. "Fine, I don't know why I asked any of this. Where are we going, Arrow?"

"I thought we'd just wander through the snow until one of the Goblin Queen's men found us."

Her heart stopped in her chest. He couldn't be so foolish, could he? They would die out here if they didn't have a plan!

"Arrow," she snarled.

He tossed his head in the air and gave away his jest early before she completely lost her mind in anger. "We're not wandering, Freya. Do you really think I'd lead us in a wild goose chase? You're with me, not Lux."

"Right," she muttered, although she was still angry he'd try to trick her like that. "Then where are we going, if you don't mind me asking?"

"There are some stones nearby that used to be in the Queen's kingdom. She liked to put magic into things that... shouldn't have magic." He stumbled over the words, almost as though someone might be listening to them. "If we find the stones, then we can likely send her a message that we're here."

"I thought you said she'd know when we were in her kingdom?"

Arrow shrugged. He lifted his brows with concern. "She should have. That's always been the Queen's way."

And in the faerie realms, something being different made everyone worried. Freya knew how this went. But why would a quest like this be easy for them? After all, the faeries weren't exactly kind to mortals. They were even less kind to the goblin kingdom.

Taking a deep breath, she plunged through the snow with a little more vigor. They needed to find these stones, that much was certain.

That damned headache came back, but she dismissed the pain. At this point, Freya was learning to live with the discomfort. She still didn't know why she was getting them, but perhaps it was being in the faerie realm that made her head ache. It would explain why her mother had avoided magic so thoroughly.

The day passed slowly. Her thighs ached with the movement of forcing herself through the thick drifts of snow. She took deep breaths to keep her breathing even, but at this point it was impossible to even do that.

They stepped into a gulley between two enormous mountains. The channel had likely been carved by water so many years ago, but now it was covered in ice that was so thick she thought it perhaps stretched all the way to the bottom of what had once been a river.

Leaning her forearm against the stone wall, she heaved in a lungful of air. "Can we take a breath?"

Arrow had his tongue out, he was breathing so hard. Sucking it back into his muzzle, he nodded. "I think a break would be well deserved at this point."

"I thought this was supposed to be easy to find?" she grumbled. "Wouldn't the Queen want people to find her? She's a damned Queen of this Court."

"Well, not anymore." Arrow sat down in the snow. A puzzled expression crossed his face as he stared at her. "No one remains in control of their Court, you see. That's impossible. You can't be the Goblin Queen and the Winter Princess at the same time."

Freya supposed that made sense. There were a lot of responsibilities that went into both positions, and she could only assume there was too much for anyone to focus on both.

She tapped the stone underneath her hand three times. "Maybe that's why she hasn't found us yet. Unrest in her own home would make sense. If she didn't want to give up either throne, then wouldn't someone be fighting her from the Winter Court?"

"Freya—"

"Arrow, this makes sense. Maybe she already has her hands full, and that's why she hasn't found us!" Freya was certain she had figured it out. Now all they had to do was find the person who was opposing the Goblin Queen. Certainly they would help in their quest.

"Freya, stop talking and look at your hand." Arrow's eyes were wide and his tail was tucked between his legs.

Oh no. What was happening now?

Freya looked down at her hand and watched as spirals of blue magic spread throughout the stone. They glowed azure and lovely. Perhaps too bright for her to look at, but she couldn't keep her eyes off the movement. The arcs of light looked like waves she used to draw in the dirt when she was little.

"What is this?" she whispered.

"The Goblin Queen's magic," Arrow replied. "That's ice magic. Only people in the Winter Court have it. I never would have guessed she was powerful enough to fill an entire mountain with her power."

Freya looked behind Arrow at the other side of the gap. "Two mountains." Even those words felt wrong to say. "Two moun-tains, Arrow."

He followed her gaze, and they both watched as the swirls began on the other mountain as well. They trailed through the stone, seemingly creating a path for them to follow.

"Do you think we should follow it?" she asked.

"I'm not sure. Magic like that isn't always a good thing." Arrow gulped. "The Goblin Queen certainly knows we're here now, though. Maybe you should take your hand off the stone."

Freya pulled her hand off the mountain. A lingering cold bit her fingers as though she'd been holding them against ice too long. Fragile blooms of frost had already coated the bottom of her hand, although they didn't sting as she thought they would.

She closed her hand into a fist. "We're here to see the Goblin Queen, so we might as well follow the path she's laid for us."

"Look out!" Arrow's shout came moments too late.

A burlap bag obscured her vision and the iron band of a meaty arm wrapped around her waist. Though she struggled against the man's grip, she realized quickly there was nothing she could do.

The Goblin Queen's men had found them.

"Arrow!" she shouted. "Arrow, where are you!"

"Fight, Freya!" His next words were garbled, likely shouted through a sack like herself.

She tried to fight, but she wasn't a warrior. Freya kicked her feet and struck back with her elbows. The man who held her made a sound like a soft snort of disapproval, and then something very hard struck the side of her head.

CHAPTER 5

She became aware of her surroundings slowly.

First, she realized there was a new kind of headache pounding through her skull. All the pain seemed to spike from a single point just above her right temple. Confusing, at first, until she remembered the sharp pain of someone striking her in the head.

Though she wasn't certain what he had hit her with, Freya knew it was something hard, round, and likely the butt of a knife. Which meant the people who had snatched them up had weapons. The Goblin Queen's personal guard? No, that made little sense.

She wiggled her wrists and found that someone had bound them behind her back. Rough rope burned the sensitive skin of her wrists, not the silken ties she might have thought a queen like this to use. That was also strange. Faeries were fond of extravagant measures, not burlap and pain.

She opened her eyes but could see nothing. The bag was still over her head. That wasn't helpful. Although, considering the temperature, she was certain she was still in the Winter Court.

The cold stone beneath her wasn't snow, so she supposed

that might be a clue. Freya wiggled a bit more, trying to get her wrists out of their bindings.

"I wouldn't do that if I were you." The voice was too soft to be intimidating. Light and airy, like snow falling in an empty field. The man's tones were eerily calming.

Freya should thank him for helping her remain steady. She needed to keep her wits about her and not panic in fear that she'd already been captured and rendered helpless. The Goblin Queen was going to think she was just a foolish mortal who lucked into beating the Goblin King.

Clearing her throat, she tried reasoning with the creature who had tied her up. "I'm here to see the Goblin Queen."

"Yes, I assumed you were trying to find your way through the kingdom when we came upon you." An intense sound followed his words. Was he sharpening a knife? "I understood you and your companion were arguing about the best way to find her. When you activated the magic, you should have known we would find you."

"I didn't know the magic was even there," she argued. "If we gave a grave offense by touching the mountain, I'd like to give my apologies personally to the queen."

Another sharp snicking sound. "I don't think the Queen would care to see you all that much. She's busy these days, you know. Running a kingdom and all that."

Should she tell him she was the mortal who had defeated the Goblin King? Freya didn't know if that would work for her or against her at this point. Maybe telling him that would make all this much worse.

But the threat of having bits of herself sliced off was enough to make her babble like an idiot. "I'd like to know where my companion is before I tell you anything else."

"The dog?" She heard metal being set down on stone, followed by approaching footsteps. "He's somewhere safe. You, however, are not somewhere safe at all."

A blast of familiar pain rocked through her skull. Not the

knife this time, but the ache that plagued her for weeks. She winced and hoped the expression was hidden behind the burlap sack.

The scent of apple pie filled her nose. A warm hand landed on her shoulder, then the heat of a breath teased her ear. Impossible, considering he'd have to be inside the sack with her, but she felt him all the same. "Tell him nothing," the Goblin King whispered. "He's going to bring you to the Queen no matter what you say."

She wasn't so certain this creature wouldn't take her fingers off one by one until she told him exactly who she was. Gulping, Freya muttered under her breath, "And what if he starts to chop me up into little pieces?"

"Then you endure." The Goblin King chuckled in her ear, obviously finding her words amusing. "But he will not harm you, Freya. His threats are empty when the Goblin Queen is interested in who you are and why you are in her kingdom."

"How do you know that?" she asked.

The heat of his presence disappeared along with the headache.

She almost swore under her breath and screamed for him to come back. Was that damned headache all his doing? She'd been fighting with it for weeks now! The pain had been unbearable in the beginning and if he was the one causing such horrific pain, she would...

Fingers snapped in front of her face, just beyond the burlap. Light filtered through the holes in the wrinkled fabric, and she could barely make out the shadowy figure of the man crouched out of her reach.

He wasn't a very large man if his outline was anything to go by. In fact, she'd call him downright willowy if she didn't also know he could hurt her.

"Focus," he said, that calming voice soothing the pain in her skull. "I need you to tell me why you're here, little girl. You are a mortal in a faerie realm. I'm sure you know you aren't very welcome."

"I'm not talking to anyone who isn't the Queen." She licked her lips and hoped the Goblin King was right. "I think she'd want to see me, and I think she'd be furious with you if I showed up in multiple pieces."

The shadow reached forward and a chilly edge of metal touched the base of her throat. "You need to talk faster, mortal woman. I'm growing weary of your games."

She was too, if the threat was sawing through the cords of her neck. Freya had never actually been threatened by a faerie before. Sure, the Spring Maiden had wanted to keep her in a drug induced stupor. The Summer Lord had been interested only in beating her with words. But neither of them had pulled a weapon and threatened to harm her physically.

Who were these feral faeries in the Winter Court?

She had to trust that the Goblin King knew what he was talking about. He'd lived in the Winter Court when he was just a young faerie. Surely he would tell her if there was something to fear.

So she mustered all the courage in her heart, gulped down the fear that shuddered through her chest, and called the faerie's bluff. "I don't think you'll hurt me at all. Not when the Goblin Queen wants to see me. And she does want to see me. I know you don't believe it, but I don't care."

"What makes you think she wants to see the likes of you?"

"You know why. Otherwise you would have left my companion and I to freeze in the snow." At least, she hoped she was right. Perhaps they liked hunting strangers down for sport. "You would have waited until we were nothing more than ice chips, like the faeries I saw the first time I was in the Winter Court."

Another voice interrupted them. This one was much deeper than the first, harsher and more direct. "You've been to the Winter Court before, mortal?"

"Yes." She took a deep breath and broke the rule the Goblin King had told her. The only thing she had to bargain with here was information, and surely this would come out before she met the Queen, anyway. "I was here to gather the essence of this court, sent by the Goblin King. This was the last piece of the puzzle I needed before I defeated him."

They immediately withdrew the blade at her throat. She could hear the faeries step away from her, then their low tones as they whispered together. She couldn't pick out any individual words, but she was certain they were arguing about what to do with her.

Good. Let them be confused about who she was and whether she was a threat to their people. A little fear would serve them right for tying her up like this.

Freya waited for them to approach her again. This time, they reached for the burlap sack around her head and yanked it off so quickly she was blinded by the bright light behind them.

Blinking through tears, she stared at the two figures and waited for them to come into focus.

The smaller one was a very slight man who looked oddly like a birch tree. The patterns were even etched into his skin, the dark streaks looking very much like a tree. His eyes were slanted almost comically, the inner points nearly touching his nose, while the outer edge winged up to his eyebrows. Those eyes were overly large as well, too big to fit his face and oddly raven-like with the dark parts swallowing the white.

The other man was larger than life. He looked like a boulder, with the dark bluish skin to boot. His stomach stretched the shirt that covered him. The buttons were so strained they looked like they might burst at any moment. He stared down at her with black eyes, no whites at all, just black. Were they brothers? Or were all the Winter Court blessed with soulless eyes?

Both of them made a rather intimidating picture that sent her heart racing in her chest.

The big one spoke first. "You are the one who defeated the Goblin King? Speak loudly, girl. This is important."

"Of course it's important," she replied, trying very hard to turn her voice haughty and warrior-like. "Untie me and bring my companion back. Then, perhaps, I'll speak with your Queen about this. But I have no interest in speaking to two lowly guards who were sent to the very outer edges of the Queen's domain."

They looked at each other, then back to her. "How would you know any of that?"

Guessing, really. That was the only way she would know. But they were both ragged looking, and their clothing had frays at the seams. The frozen faeries she'd seen around that icy snowflake had been delicate. Lovely. Their clothing was impeccable and their faces smooth.

These two had pock marked skin and the larger one had spots of peeling flakes where the sun had burned him. If they were living a life that difficult, then they certainly weren't high in the rankings of guards.

She leaned forward dramatically. "I'll speak well of your treatment and how you tricked me. You just have to bring me to the Queen and I'm certain she would let you return from your exile."

"This isn't an exile," the thin one replied with an angry grunt. He reached into his pocket and pulled the knife out again. "I should take your eyes for suggesting such a thing, mortal. You are beneath us."

"Mind, body, and soul far lesser than you," she said. "I'm certain that you think I'm beneath you, but I was the one who defeated the Goblin King. Was I not?"

Freya would have looked at her nails in the silence that followed. At least that body language would have made her appear confident and unafraid. But her shoulders were aching from being tied up for so long, and she'd lost all feeling in her fingers. Her entire body screamed for her to do something, anything that would get her free. And yet, she was at the mercy of these two idiots.

They looked at each other again, and the big one nodded to the back of the cave. They skittered away to whisper in each other's ears. Their hushed tones filled the cave with a sound like trickling water. Freya stared up at the ceiling and prayed for patience.

She'd need more than a little to deal with these two nitwits.

Finally, the smaller one approached her with a frown on his face. "Prove it."

"Prove what?"

"That you were the one to defeat the Goblin King. Everyone knows he's fallen, so you could just be some mortal woman looking to manipulate our queen in the hopes she'll give you enough gold to make you a princess in your land." He scratched his groin, then sniffed his fingers. "We need a little more than just your word."

She tilted her head to the side and smiled, trying to remain pretty and not just angry. "Your entire court gathers their magic from a snowflake that had magic poured into it. It looks like glass, but it's just a snowflake. And your queen has the Goblin King locked up in a prison because she can't let him go. Oh, and all the faeries were frozen in a war. That's why you hate the Goblin King. He did it to you, and the Queen will stop at nothing to punish him for what he did."

She said too much. Far too much. The two guards in front of her weren't involved in the war. If they had fought, they would have died due to some foolish mistake. None of what she said would make any sense to the two of them.

But the big one shrugged and said, "Would she know any of that if she was just a mortal?"

"I don't know."

"Well, I don't either." The big one narrowed his eyes and pointed at her with a meaty hand. "If you're lying, then I'm going to pull all your limbs off your body. One by one."

Freya ground her teeth. "If you did that, then I would die. I'd like very much to stay alive, so I can assure you, none of this is a lie."

"We'll see about that." He stalked toward her, lifted her by a bound arm, and gave her a shake. "Why don't we bring both you and your companion to the queen, eh? She'll know what to do with you."

"I think that's a fabulous idea." Except, now she didn't want to do that at all.

If these two were what the Winter Court faeries were like, then what kind of monster was their queen?

CHAPTER 6

The two faerie thugs dragged her down the crag where she'd first seen winter magic and out into another frozen tundra. They gathered up Arrow who had been tied like a prized hog and then left waiting for them in a snowbank.

He growled when the smaller man reached for his ties. "If you touch me, I will bite your fingers off."

"Arrow," Freya said. "Let them untie you. They're taking us to see the queen."

Arrow's eyes widened in surprise, but he didn't snap at the birch faerie's fingers when he reached for the ties again. The faerie made quick work of the ropes and then lunged away from Arrow as he rolled onto his feet and gave a swift shake.

He quickly trotted to Freya's side. "I don't know why we have these thugs taking us, anyway. They seem decidedly untrustworthy."

"More trustworthy than a goblin," the big one grumbled.

"Debatable," Freya replied with a chuckle. "You tied the two of us up without asking who we are. The goblins gave me a much better greeting than that."

The birch faerie stared at her with those blank, odd eyes. "How did they greet you?"

"With dinner." A soft smile curved over her face as she remembered the food and the madness. "Their children greeted me and I waded into the fray to tame the wild beasts. They gave me food and drink, and memories I could never forget."

She hoped the softness in her voice met Arrow's ears. In a way, it was her apology to him.

The goblins weren't the monsters she'd thought them to be for such a long time. And Freya had a lot of apologizing to do for demonizing them for so many years. All she could hope for was that her words would at least take a small step toward easing the rift between them.

Arrow met her gaze with a soft expression, then blinked his long lashes. "You left a lasting impression on the little ones. They still ask about you, you know. Terrible little beasts, but they want to talk about the pretty mortal lady who picked them up by the scruff of their necks."

The birch faerie snorted. "They won't be asking much longer. They'll have a lot worse things to deal with when the Goblin Queen finally takes over all the kingdoms."

So, that was her plan then. The Queen would take over everything Freya knew and admired, because a Goblin royal had a right to all of the courts. The King or Queen was more powerful than any court leader. That fact had been drilled into Freya's mind.

Blowing out a long breath, she wiggled her fingers behind her back. If she could get out of these bindings, that would be a huge step toward controlling this situation.

"Where are we going?" she asked, trying to distract them from her movements.

"To the Queen, of course." The larger faerie pointed down a cave tunnel that disappeared into the icy tundra before them. "If you don't mind going first, that is. You've been very brave thus far, mortal. Let's test just how brave you are."

Far braver than he gave her credit for, apparently. Freya was ready to get this over with.

She plunged through the snow and into the tunnel that disappeared deep under the mountains. At first, she couldn't see very well. Then light bloomed in the walls.

Thick slabs of ice surrounded them. The Goblin Queen's magic ran through all the frozen walls, turning them a bright, deep blue. The light pulsed brighter, then dimmed, as though it had a heartbeat that she couldn't hear but could see.

This wasn't frightening, even though the faeries had intended it to be scary. It was beautiful, yes, and a wonderful display of the Goblin Queen's power. But not frightening.

Freya held her head high and continued deeper into the heart of the mountain. The floor was slick with ice, but she struggled her way without falling. Freya's heart beat with fear because she knew she wouldn't be able to catch herself if she fell. Her arms were useless tied behind her back.

The birch faerie snickered behind her. "Looks like you've never walked on ice before, mortal."

"I've walked on ice with skates," she snarled. "Or perhaps even with solid boots, but never down a slope made entirely of ice. How are you doing this without falling?"

He grabbed her shoulder and spun her around. She blew out an angry breath, but looked at his foot that he brandished in the air. Four toes, four long claws that dug into the ice wherever he walked.

The faerie bared his teeth in a sinister grin. "I'm made to stroll through these halls, mortal. Are you?"

"Obviously not."

She continued until the slope was so steep that she had to stop. The tunnel extended down into darkness as the light slowly disappeared in the distance. She wondered why it wasn't still glowing down there.

"You have to keep going," the birch faerie said. "We'll leave you here."

"I don't think the Queen would like that." Freya gulped down the spike of fear. If they left her here, she wasn't sure she could climb back out. Her boots would slip and eventually she would fall.

She imagined herself tumbling into the darkness, sliding uncontrollably until she hit a wall. She might live. Or she might bash her head against the ice and die here in the darkness, alone.

The bigger faerie walked by her with a snort. "Not so brave after all, are we?"

He took one step onto the sloping ice and then disappeared. Or rather, he fell onto the ice gracefully for his size and slid down into the darkness without another word. She didn't even hear him as he plummeted into the shadows.

How? How could he do that without having a second thought?

"You next, goblin," the birch faerie snarled.

"Absolutely not." Arrow took a step back while shaking his head. "I'll go when Freya goes."

"Is that the mortal's name?" The birch faerie looked her up and down with that disgusting grin on his face. "Good to know what your name is, my dear. I wonder all the different ways I might be able to use it."

She hoped not to curse her. Her mother had said faeries could do that. All they needed was a name and they could force anyone to do whatever they wanted. Even turn her into something else, like a toad or rat.

Arrow bared his teeth with a snarl and stepped in front of her. "You wouldn't dare."

"I sure would. Especially if she doesn't show up at the bottom with us." The birch faerie reached for Arrow, scooped him up, and then slid into the shadows as well.

Then it was just Freya. She stood with her hands still tied behind her back, staring into what felt like the end of all she knew. How could she do this? She wasn't so brave as to dive into the unknown. What if she landed on shards of ice that impaled her? This could all be some kind of trick from the faeries, and then she was finally out of their hair for good.

"You're afraid of this, but you weren't afraid to make a deal with the Goblin King." His voice soothed the ache in her soul.

This was someone she knew how to deal with. Freya had already defeated the Goblin King. She knew how to manipulate him, or at the very least, she knew what was expected of her.

The Goblin King wanted someone to spar with him. He wanted a verbal joust where she could best him or be beaten. It didn't matter what the result was in the end. He just wanted her to challenge him.

She licked her lips and said, "You were far less terrifying than potentially plummeting to my death."

"But you faced death multiple times while trying to beat me. You might not remember it like that, but you did." He materialized within the ice to her left. Or perhaps not within it, but reflected upon it. Like a mirror. "I find I don't like this version of you that can feel fear."

She snorted. "Sorry to disappoint you, Goblin King."

"Please." He rolled his eyes. "No matter what you do, I highly doubt you could disappoint me, Freya. You were the greatest adversary I've ever battled. And I'm impressed you've come this far. You could have run."

She curled her fingers into tight fists, digging her nails into the palms of her hands until she felt the slightest prick of pain. "Are you really here?" She had to know the truth. "Or are you some figment of my imagination to help me get through all this?"

"Does it matter?" His mouth turned down at the edges and fine lines furrowed between his brows. He was saddened by her words, almost as though he didn't want her to know the truth.

"Of course it matters," she whispered. "I need to know if I'm alone right now or if you're here with me."

"Freya," he scolded. "Would it really make you feel better to know that I was here with you? I'm your enemy, remember? The villain in your story that tried to stop you from getting your sister back. The bad guy shouldn't turn into the one who consoles you in your hour of need."

"I'm asking you to." She took a deep breath and felt her nostrils flair with panic. "I'm asking you to take off your mask of bad guy and villain. Help me, Eldridge."

A shiver traveled through his entire body, rocking his shoulders at the sound of his own name. The darkness in his eyes deepened and those swirling silver stars seemed to glow brighter. "Jump, Freya. I need you to find me."

And then he disappeared again, fading from view like he was never there at all.

She felt something deep inside her stomach twist. Quietly she asked, "Eldridge?"

The word fell in the cold air, disappointing and lacking in life. He was gone. The Goblin King had left her in the cold, all alone, to make this decision on her own.

She shivered in the dark with the strange blue light lighting up the world behind her. "Come back," she whispered. The words choked in her throat as sobs pushed their way to the surface. "Even if you aren't real or just a dream, please come back."

No one answered her. This choice was hers and hers alone, even though the Goblin King had tried to tell her what to do. He wanted her to leap into the darkness without fear. She wasn't a bird who could fly, though, and that fear had been buried deep in her chest since all of this had started.

Now was the time to prove that she was brave.

She straightened her shoulders and tensed the muscles of her back. Awkwardly, she turned around so her back was to the darkness because she refused to slide into the shadows face first. Then she got onto her knees, flopped onto her belly, and let the ice take her away.

Arctic wind blasted through her hair and ice tore at the front of her cloak. The sound of the woolen fabric ripping could barely be heard over her wild tumble. Freya told herself not to scream. Even if this was the end of her life, she would not give these monstrous faeries the satisfaction of hearing her scream.

Then, she hit a flat portion of the ice and rolled to a stop. Her arms felt like they had been torn apart, but at least the feeling in them had returned.

Wincing, she tried to wiggle onto her back without success.

"Well, that was dramatic," the birch faerie said. His hands grasped the ropes around her wrists and he hauled her onto her feet. Settling her with a jerk, he shook her hard. "Are you still alive?"

Though she was peering through the tangled mass of her hair, she still nodded. "I'm alive."

"Pity," he snarled. "I would have liked you better dead. Come on, then. The Queen is in the throne room."

Freya muttered underneath her breath the same thing she'd said to the Goblin King. "Sorry to disappoint."

CHAPTER 7

The two faeries dragged Freya through countless icy halls until they stopped before doors that were three stories high. These white, iced doors were carved with a scene from what looked like a battle. A hundred elves at the bottom level all pointed their sharpened spears up at a monster that looked like a dragon. A single woman stood before the creature with her arms outstretched.

A crown topped her head, and Freya could only assume this woman was meant to be the Goblin Queen herself. But why would she welcome a creature so fearsome as a dragon? Especially when the rest of her people were pointing their weapons at the terrifying beast?

Freya didn't have time to ask questions. The two faeries busted through the doors and shoved her onto her knees. She fell onto her hands and knees, sliding across the ice until she stopped before the stairs.

She would not show fear. Not when the Goblin Queen was likely a very astute woman and would notice any weakness. Freya had to pretend that she was here seeking an audience with the Queen because she wanted recognition for her actions. Not because she was searching for the King.

The cold bit into her fingers and palms. Her breath fogged in front of her face. She stared down at the blue ice of the floor and counted to ten. Only then, when she was certain her expression wouldn't give her away, did she look up.

Freya let her eyes feast upon the sight of the throne room.

Stained glass windows, or perhaps colored ice, turned the walls into a rainbow of overwhelming vibrance. The stairs led up to a throne made entirely of jagged icicles and snow. The arms were carved into twin bears that held the Goblin Queen's throne aloft.

And seated on that throne was the Goblin Queen herself. A pale blue gown floated around her form, carefully laced with individual snowflakes stitched so perfectly, Freya had to wonder if they were actually snow. Her fingers were white, not just pale, but completely white with long pointed nails. The same crown that was carved on the doors sat on her head. Three spikes of ice, like the ones that had dripped from Freya's windows when she was a little girl.

On her face, she wore a mask made of tiny icicles, each creating a beautiful pattern that surrounded her blinding blue eyes.

The Goblin Queen stared down at her with an expression of apathy. "Who is this? Why did you bring a mortal to my throne room?"

The two faeries behind Freya lunged forward, each talking over the other.

"We found her and the dog in the caverns, my queen. They were trespassing on your lands and we thought you'd like to see them," the big one said.

"She said she's the one who beat the Goblin King, and that she wanted to see you. I can't imagine that she did, I mean look at her, but you said you wanted to know who had managed to..." the thin one babbled until the Goblin Queen pointed at him with a sharpened nail.

"You," she snarled. "Say that again."

The birch faerie gulped. "She said she was the one who beat the Goblin King, and that she needed to speak with you immediately."

Freya watched all this happen as if she wasn't even in the room. No one was looking at her or Arrow, who she assumed was somewhere behind them. Freya kept her eyes on the most important person in the room. The Queen.

The Goblin Queen's eyes had narrowed suspiciously, but she still wasn't looking at the mortal on her knees before the throne. Instead, she eyed the faeries as though they were something disgusting she had stepped on.

"Are you certain?" she asked.

The birch faerie looked at the bigger one, then back to the Queen. "Certain of what, my lady?"

"Certain that this measly mortal was the one to defeat the greatest Goblin King this realm has ever seen?"

"Uh," the birch faerie gulped again. His throat worked hard before he whispered, "There's no way to know that for certain, my lady."

"Then it's a shame you thought the risk of wasting my time was more important than the reward you might get." She snapped her fingers. "I don't want to see you in my sight again. You've outlasted your worth."

The birch faerie's eyes widened in horror. He dropped onto his knees, begging, "Please, my lady. I will prove my worth to you! All I'm asking is—"

He didn't have time to say anything else. The frost spread up from the icy floor into his skin. He screamed in pain as the cold froze him solid, but there was nothing he could do to fight against the Goblin Queen's magic. Freya didn't know how long it took for him to solidify. She held her breath the entire time, so it couldn't have taken very long.

The silence that came after shocked her to the very core. His last scream had been one of pain and anguish, but nothing could be done to help him. Not even the big faerie moved, and certainly not his queen.

The Goblin Queen lifted a hand and stared at her nails. "Such a pity your friend wasn't more useful. Perhaps you will find your path to be a little less reliant on hope. Do I make that clear?"

Freya watched the big faerie nod firmly, but his eyes remained on his poor partner. Frozen to the floor with his hands raised forever, pleading with his Queen for mercy.

The Queen stood from her throne and stepped down the stairs. Her skirts swished around her legs, the sound so soft it almost made her forget the horrible thing the Queen had just done.

She strode past Freya without a glance. No, she approached the frozen figure instead.

With a gentle hand, she smoothed her palm over his face. "You were one of my favorites," she told the frozen figure. "This hurts me so much more than it hurts you."

The Goblin Queen planted a hand on the birch faerie's chest and shoved.

He fell almost as though time had slowed. It took a very long time for the icy figure to meet the ground. But the instant the ice hit the floor, it shattered into a thousand bright red pieces. Like rubies someone had tipped out of a jeweler's box.

Freya hissed out a low breath and flinched. She looked away from the horrific sight of a body in so many pieces. That had been a faerie just moments ago. He'd been alive and while he'd been terrifying, he hadn't deserved to die just because he'd done what he was supposed to. Bring the woman who had defeated the Goblin King to the new Queen.

The soft hush of falling snow approached from her left. Freya watched out of the corner of her eye as the Goblin Queen reached out a hand for Freya to take. "Rise, mortal."

Freya should have taken the offered hand. She should have at least tried her best to play along with this morbid game, but she couldn't. She stood on her own and kept her eyes straight ahead.

The Goblin Queen scoffed. "You can act all high and mighty, mortal. But you are not a magical creature. If I wanted to destroy you just as I destroyed him, then I would. Right now, I want to know if you were lying as your kind is so famous for."

"I was not lying," she replied. "I beat the Goblin King at his own game. He kidnapped my sister, and I would have done anything to get her safely home."

"Your sister?" The Goblin Queen stepped around her and stood so Freya was forced to look into her unnatural eyes. "I don't see a sister with you."

"I didn't bring her here."

"Why not?"

The questions were making her head spin. How was she supposed to keep all these lies in order? Freya was going to forget something and then she would ruin the entire plan. All she had to do was... Well, not lie that much. But bend the truth into a little lie she could remember.

For once, Freya was glad she didn't bring Esther with her.

"She wanted to go home," Freya replied. "To the mortal realm with all the rest of our people."

"And you?" The Goblin Queen watched her without blinking. "Why are you still here?"

What would Esther have said? Freya cleared her throat and answered as her sister would have. "I like it here. There is more in the faerie realm for me than in the mortal realm. However, I wanted to come and meet you once I heard that my heroic deeds had freed you and your people. I thought, perhaps, you would be grateful."

That sparked some interest in the queen's eyes. The Goblin Queen blinked, finally, and then reached up to remove her mask.

The queen was a beautiful woman underneath all that ice. Her eyes were not too large for her head, although they were certainly larger than most. Framed with dark, long lashes, they were set into a heart-shaped face that most women would have killed for. Bright, berry red lips stood out in stark contrast to her pale skin. Removing the mask allowed the spiral curls of her white hair to fall around her face as well. Perfect, as Freya would have expected.

A long sigh spilled from the Queen's lips. "If you really were the one who defeated the king, then tell me. What did you do to beat him?"

"He sent me to all the courts to gather the essence of each. I obtained perfume from the Spring Maiden. A sprig of lavender in a spell bottle from the Summer Lord. A portrait from the Autumn Thief." Freya paused for dramatic effect and then added, "And I figured out that the Goblin King was the essence of this court."

The Goblin Queen's eyes widened with each thing Freya said until finally she burst into laughter at the last part. "Ah yes, he is so vain as to not think you would have figured that out. Clever girl. Perhaps you were the one who defeated him after all."

"I am." Freya glanced over at the red ice chips behind the queen and then resolved herself to one last lie. "My name is Esther, my queen. It was my hopes that you would feel some sort of... gratefulness for my part in freeing you and your people from your prison."

The Queen tucked her hands behind her back and nodded. "So you want something from me, is that it?"

"Just a place in your court for a while. I wish to learn more about this faerie realm, and I do not want to remain in any of the others." Freya swallowed hard and hoped that action looked like mere nerves.

"A place in my court is frequently sought after by more impressive people than you." This time, the Queen's eyes shifted to the side. Almost as though she was the one lying.

But that wasn't possible. Faeries couldn't lie, that was the one thing that had always given her a leg up over the Goblin King.

Unless this one was different.

Freya took a deep breath and plunged into the unknown. "My companion and I hoped we would be welcome here after all the good we've done for you and your people. After all. Without me, you would still be frozen."

The Goblin Queen's expression was calculating. She suspected Freya was lying, although there was no way for Freya to know if the Queen realized that her name was a lie or if she knew there were many layers to this lie.

Finally, the Queen lifted a delicate shoulder. "My darling, of course you are welcome here. You are the only one to ever defeat the Goblin King. I'm impressed a mere mortal could do so, but I'm also happy that you did."

Happy was good. That was a start. She could work with that, even though the expression on the Queen's face made it appear the happiness was tenuous at best.

Not to mention the dead body behind her.

Freya blew out a soft breath. "Thank you, my queen. It's an honor to know that I have pleased you."

The Queen snorted, "Yes, they all say that. But since you were the one to release me, I wish to give you a gift. A token of my appreciation."

All she could hope was that the gift wasn't like the Spring Maiden's gift. Faeries were always spinning things into their own desires, and if this Queen wanted to put Freya into a stupor, then she would realize rather quickly that Freya was not so easy to trick.

Narrowing her gaze, Freya crossed her arms over her chest and nodded. "A gift is always appreciated if it's given with good intent."

The Queen chuckled again. "You have dealt with faeries before, I see. You don't trust me. That's smart. But my gifts rarely have teeth, my dear. You can see I don't hide my displeasure behind falsehoods and ridiculous tactics. This gift is one of thanks, and it will be the only one I give you in return."

"Then I will take the gift."

"Stay in my castle with me." The Queen lifted a brow, surveying Freya's reactions. "Esther, as you call yourself, I think you would make a lovely addition to my court. I'd like you to stay close. I'm curious about your opinions of my court and the people within it. If you could beat the Goblin King so easily, I'm certain you have more use than as only a passing visitor."

That would do. Freya could work with that.

She dropped into an awkward curtsey. "It would be my pleasure, your highness."

"Oh no." The Queen's voice dropped into a low growl. "I assure you, the pleasure is all mine."

<h1 style="text-align:center">CHAPTER 8</h1>

The Queen dismissed Freya with a wave of her hand. The gesture summoned a small, pale creature who detached itself from the ice and stepped toward her.

The little monster looked like it was made entirely out of ice. Perhaps as if it were a doll the Goblin Queen used to play with when she was little. Its feet were forever pointed into little high heels that clicked on the floor. Its hair was frost, creating a different color on top of its head, and its eyes were frozen within the water sloshing in its skull. The strange orbs moved through the liquid of its cranium freely, sometimes gathering together, sometimes far apart.

It teetered over to the throne room door, then lifted an icy hand. Waving as if it wanted her to follow it.

Though the beast was strange, she didn't want to stay in the throne room any longer than she had to. The dead body was the only barrier between her and the door. Freya stepped through the red ice and winced as a piece crunched underneath her boot.

The little monster didn't notice at all. Or if it did, it didn't react.

Arrow waited for her with wide eyes and his nose sniffing the air. When she walked by him and touched a hand to his head, he nudged against her warmth. "Well done, mortal."

"Thank you," she whispered. "I thought I blew it a few times there."

"Unlikely. The Queen is curious about you, and that's the best start you could have asked for." He chuffed out a breath of disbelief. "And now we're staying in the castle. Exactly where we need to be."

"Shh," Freya scolded. "We have no idea if the walls have ears here. Unless you want to end up like our friend back there."

Arrow shuddered. "No, I think neither of us wants to meet the same fate. You're right. We'll wait until we can ward our rooms."

Whatever that meant. Freya didn't know the first thing about magic.

They followed the ice creature down through so many halls she was immediately turned around. Freya had no idea how big this castle was, or just how deep into the heart of the mountain it disappeared. It seemed as though they walked forever before the creature turned and pointed to a blank spot in the wall.

Freya cleared her throat. "Am I supposed to walk through the ice?"

The creature rolled its eyes, then waved a hand. A small handle appeared on the ice where it pointed, followed by a screeching sound as the ice cracked in an uneven shape of a door.

Was she supposed to stay there? Freya could just barely see through the warped glass, and the room inside appeared to be filled with snow drifts. "I can't stay here," she said. "I'm mortal. I'll freeze."

It blinked a few times, then made a sound like broken glass. The creature toddled off, and Freya didn't know if she was supposed to follow it or not.

She looked down at Arrow. "Are we going with it again or..."

"It's going to bring you blankets," he replied. "I'm to follow the creature because I have a separate room."

Her stomach turned. "What? No, you will not stay anywhere else. You're staying with me."

He looked up at her with soulful eyes. "I don't think we have a choice, Freya."

Of course there was a choice. There was always a choice, and she didn't want him to go with the ice monster where they had no idea what the creature's plan was for Arrow. She needed him to stay with her because he was the only thing holding her together. Who else would she talk to?

"Arrow," she hissed. "Don't go with it."

The creature stopped at the end of the hallway and made the sound of broken glass again.

Arrow sighed heavily and shook his head. "I don't have a choice, Freya. There are no choices in the Winter Court. We do what the Goblin Queen says, remember? I will be safe."

He reached up and nudged her hand with his nose, and she felt something brittle slide into her hand. A small piece of paper rolled up that he'd been holding in his mouth. When had he gotten this?

Freya closed both her hands into fists and nodded. "Fine, then. But be careful. I can't lose you too."

He gave her an odd look, and she knew it was partly because he didn't believe her. So much between them still needed to be fixed, and she hadn't the faintest idea how to fix it.

Freya stayed in the hallway until the two of them disappeared from sight. Obviously the creature wasn't worried about her wandering around the castle. There were no doors for her to open, not without knowing how to make the door knobs appear. So if she wanted to wander, she was likely free to do so. But Freya would eventually freeze solid and die somewhere in a hallway no one traversed.

She turned and opened the door to her own room rather than tempt that fate.

The interior was rather bland. Just a bed made of ice in the corner, overly large but lacking any blankets. A fireplace carved out of snow, not exactly helpful considering the entire thing would melt. And twin snowdrifts in the back that looked like they might be mounded over chairs.

She glanced around to make sure no one was looking, then unrolled Arrow's note.

"Repeat these words, Freya. It will ward the room from the Goblin Queen's spying. Imagine in your mind a golden bubble forming around this room and this room only."

Was she supposed to perform magic? This was a spell.

She crumpled the paper in her fist again and sighed. He knew she was just a mortal. Freya couldn't do magic. She just couldn't.

A knock on the door startled her. Spinning on her heel, Freya pressed her fist to her heart and watched as the ice creature walked through the door. It held a mound of blankets and sheepskin in its arms. Without a word, it dumped the skins on the floor, then pointed at the fireplace.

Then it made that sound again.

"I can't understand you," she said.

The creature's eyes rolled in the block of its head, then it made another horrible sound and walked back out the door. Through the ice, as though there wasn't a barrier there at all.

Freya turned away with a sigh and stared down at the furs. They were a start to keep her warm, but she wasn't sure how much they would do. Her cheeks already stung in the cold and she desperately wanted to take off all these layers.

No fire. No warmth. She could go to sleep and freeze overnight, passing into the realm of the dead in a peaceful manner, but far too soon.

She had to sleep, though. Especially since her last rest was in a rocking chair. So she stooped down and picked up the spell from the floor. Unrolling it, she cleared her throat.

"I clear this room of all ill intent and spying ears. By the power of the Autumn Court, I banish any energy that might wish to cause me harm. Only those with pure intent may enter these walls." Freya finished and squeezed her eyes shut, thinking of a bright bubble expanding through the room.

Golden light, she thought. Golden light that no one else could get through.

Connecting with the spell was easier than she thought, but she opened one eye and it didn't look like anything was happening. Squeezing them shut again, Freya tried her best.

Finally, she shook her head and tucked the paper into her pocket. "This is ridiculous."

She couldn't do spell work. Trying was just a waste of her time. She set about getting the furs onto the icy block of the floor, trying to cover every bit that her body might touch and then laying the blankets on top.

Already shivering with anticipation of the chilly rest, she rubbed her arms. "This will have to do."

Freya laid down and pulled the blankets high over her shoulders. What she wouldn't have given for a proper fire, not just a cold fireplace carved into the snow. Not the semblance of warmth with none of the reassurance. This place was far colder than she'd thought. And now she was wondering if the Goblin Queen was more of a match than she'd expected.

Sure, the Goblin King had fallen to her wit. But he'd wanted to fall.

She tucked the blanket up to her nose and tried her best to drift off to sleep. And she must have, because when she opened her eyes again there was a fire crackling in the fireplace. The flames merrily danced in the marble carved frame. The snow had melted off the carvings, revealing the real room beneath it.

A dull throb of a headache pounded behind her eyes and then disappeared in the next instant.

The heat distracted her so much that it took awhile for her to notice where the actual heat was coming from.

Stretched out beside her, resting on the ice as though it were a bed, lay the Goblin King. His head was turned toward the flames, the cords of his neck silhouetted by the red light of the fire. His bare chest gleamed, although she didn't know how he could be comfortable while shirtless, sprawled out on ice.

"What—" she started to sit up, only to pause when he looked at her with those dark, soulful eyes.

The Goblin King raised a finger and pressed it against his lips. "Shh, Freya. We don't know who might be listening."

She braced herself on one arm and stared down at him in shock. "You're in my bedroom."

"Don't be so obtuse. Of course I'm in your bedroom, Freya." He shook his head in disappointment, then looked back at the fire.

"No, I just..." Arguing with him would get her nowhere. The Goblin King was a strange man, and if he wanted to be here in her bedroom, then apparently that's where he was going to be. Freya sank back down onto the blanket she'd bundled up as a pillow. "I warded the room. Arrow gave me the spell."

"And you did a good job of it for someone who claims magic doesn't run in her family." The firelight played over the strands of his dark hair, ragged and fallen out of place. "But your mother said the same thing when I first saw her. Magic doesn't always run in bloodlines, Freya. It runs in the heart."

Her own heart thudded frantically at what he had suggested. He'd seen her mother? Did that mean maybe... Maybe her parents were alive?

Licking her lips, she asked, "You knew my mother? You never told me that."

He tilted his head to look at her, then pressed his finger to his lips again. "We cannot talk about it here, Freya. Soon. Soon, I will tell you everything I know."

She was so tired of that answer. He always promised that, and somehow he'd get himself into yet another position where he could tell her nothing. She opened her mouth to argue with him further.

"No arguing," he interrupted. "Your ward was well

constructed, but that doesn't mean they're infallible. Soon, Freya. But for now, just pretend that I'm here. And maybe that you don't mind that I'm here."

Freya might have insisted on an argument if she hadn't noticed a strange light in his eyes. Leaning closer, she paused only when his breath fanned across her lips. She wasn't going to kiss him, although he might have thought she would. Instead, she was looking at the reflection in his dark eyes.

She could see herself, but not the room. Behind her own reflection she could see cold stone walls, stalactites hanging from the ceiling, and bars that gleamed red hot. Everything else was iced over and as she stared, a drop of water hit one of the bars and sizzled. Boiling instantly.

"You aren't really here, are you?" she whispered. "Where are you, Goblin King? How can I find you?"

He slowly lifted his hand toward her face, giving her plenty of time to back away.

She didn't.

The Goblin King cupped her jaw and let out a long, relieved sigh. "I can't tell you where I am. But you are correct, I'm not really here. I had hoped tonight we could pretend I was, though. Just for a few moments."

He was in some kind of prison, she knew that. But she didn't know where the Goblin Queen had her prison. She didn't even know if there was one in the Winter Court, or if he was somewhere far out of her reach.

Frustration boiled in her blood. "Why can't you tell me where you are?"

The Goblin King tugged her in his grip, forcing her to come ever closer to his face. His eyes drifted shut. Long lashes dusted his cheeks that were too hollow. "Just for the night, Freya. I want to pretend that I'm not where I am. That you are really here with me and that I am not alone."

Perhaps there would be another time for her to argue with him. Freya gave in and let her forehead fall to press against his.

The warmth of his skin burned through hers, almost as though magic spread between them.

A long sigh blasted over her lips. The Goblin King cleared his throat and gruffly said, "I wish you'd call me Eldridge, you know. After all, we've been through, I think you've earned that."

"It feels strange."

"Why?" he whispered.

"If I call you by your name, then it's like we're friends." Freya strangely felt as though she were baring her soul to him. Like she'd ripped open her chest and hoped he liked what she hid underneath. "And we aren't friends. You're still the monster who stole my sister away from her home. The creature who convinced me to come to the faerie realm and lose everything that I love."

"And yet, you're still here. Still trying to save me, even though I'm the villain in your story." He rocked his head from side to side, smoothing his skin against hers. "I have a strange request for you, enemy of mine. I hope you have enough compassion in your heart to pity an evil goblin."

She didn't.

She shouldn't.

Freya knew he was a horrible creature who had done horrible things. She'd read his diary with his history and knew he'd fought in faerie wars that silenced so many, even though he was trying to save them.

She knew a thousand times over that he didn't deserve her pity.

"What do you need, Eldridge?" she murmured. "Only for tonight."

"And then you'll hate me again," he replied with a deep chuckle.

"What other feelings should I have for you? No others. Anything else would surely name me a mad woman." The question was the truth, but tears burned in her eyes after saying them.

His hand shifted from her jaw. Fingers spreading through her hair, he cupped the back of her neck and drew her down into the curve of his body. He settled her head against his shoulder, her torso draped over his. And with another heaving sigh, Eldridge lifted his other hand and clasped her hand to his heart. "Touch me, Freya. Just for the night. You can go back to hating me whenever you want, but I need to feel alive. I need to feel something other than cold."

She stiffened before she realized he meant nothing untoward. He wasn't moving her hand. He wasn't trying to start anything at all.

The Goblin King simply wanted her to rest on his heart and hold him. That was all. He wanted to feel another living person against his heart and listen to the steady rhythm of her breath.

Her resolve shattered like that poor faerie who had died in the throne room. A thousand pieces. All scattered around her like stars in the sky.

Nodding, she tucked herself closer into the crook of his body and eased her full weight down onto him. "You've had a trying time of it. I understand."

A deep rumble echoed in her ear. "A trying time of it. Yes, I suppose you could call it that."

"Only for the night," she repeated.

"Of course. I'd expect nothing less from the conqueror of the Goblin King." His hand in her hair shifted down her neck and back, resting finally on the curve of her hip.

As they both drifted into sleep, Freya whispered against his shoulder, "I'm going to find you, you know. This isn't forever."

His hand tightened on her waist. "I know, Freya. I have every hope that you will once again succeed."

CHAPTER 9

Freya woke to cold air and icy floors. Her body shivered her out of the dreaming realm and shook her into the present. Sitting up, she rubbed her hands up and down her arms to try to warm up.

She'd been warm last night, hadn't she? There had been a fire in that fireplace that was iced over once again. As if her meeting with Eldridge had been nothing more than a dream.

But that wasn't possible. She remembered him right next to her. He'd been here, and she'd been resting against his warm chest.

Freya flexed her hands, remembering the feeling of his smooth chest rising and falling underneath them. Her cheeks flamed. She'd laid on the Goblin King, even snuggled in close, and that was apparently fine in the moment?

What had she been thinking!

Freya palmed her head and sighed. Why in the world would she have ever allowed him to do that? She should have been screaming at him for even trying to lie beside her, let alone insist that she touch him. Her mother must be rolling over in her grave.

The mother that Eldridge said he had known. That he'd talked to and even hinted that her mother had performed magic.

Yet another reason she had to get the Goblin King out of this prison. Freya had a thousand questions for him to answer, and he would answer them no matter what. If she had to tie him down in a prison of her own making, then so be it. He would give her the answers she so desperately sought.

Then she heard the tip tapping sound of an ice creature walking down the hall. Not a single second would be her own, it seemed. The Goblin Queen's monster walked through the wall without bothering to knock.

She stared, then blinked a few times to clear the grit of sleep from her eyes. "Did you learn how to talk in the time you've been gone?"

"Yes." The creature's voice was still rough and horrible to listen to, but at least it knew her language. "Follow me."

Though she wanted to argue, Freya stumbled to her feet. Her hair was plastered to one side of her head and her clothing was now horribly wrinkled. How long had she been wearing this dress and woolen coat?

Don't think about it, she told herself. She could meet a Goblin Queen in grubby clothing and the woman shouldn't complain. If the Queen wanted her to visit looking like some kind of visiting royalty, then she needed to provide Freya with new clothing.

And it could only be the Queen who wanted her. Why else would this creature be here?

"Where are we going?" she asked, striding toward the door.

"The Queen would like to have breakfast with you."

Ah yes, breakfast. As a normal Queen would want to do.

Freya felt like this was a trap. She needed to prepare for anything. If her previous dealings with faeries were anything to go by, then this was yet another trick to get more information out of her.

As she strode through the blue, icy halls, Freya reminded

herself of the lies she'd already told the Queen. She was Esther, not Freya. Her sister had gone back to the mortal realm while Freya had stayed here, because she preferred the faerie realm.

Were there any others? She didn't think so, but this was what she had worried about. Too many lies were difficult to keep track of, and this Queen was intelligent. She'd sense any weakness in Freya and pounce on it like a viper on a mouse.

They didn't go to the throne room this time, although they passed by the horrific doors. Freya swallowed hard when she saw the dragon again. Hopefully those weren't still alive or, if she was lucky, that they hadn't been real at all.

The ice creature's footsteps echoed through the halls, and Freya swore they sounded like the ticking of a clock. A clock that was ticking down to the next time when she would have to face the Goblin Queen. So she steeled herself for the battle that was to come.

They stopped in front of a new doorway that consisted of twisted ice coiling up to the ceiling. Ribbons, she realized. They were ribbons falling down as if some lovely lady had just pulled them off her dress.

What a strange place. The beauty of it was incredible, however, it was also terrifying in its construction. Every detail of this castle had clearly been made with magic that was unfathomable to her mind.

Magic that supposedly she could also use.

Gulping, Freya walked past the ice creature and into what must have once been a dining room. A waterfall of ice covered bright tapestries on the back wall. Long icicles hung from the ceiling and their ends glowed with bright, glistening lights. Snow fell through the air, even though they weren't outside. Tiny, perfect snowflakes danced as they fell.

A silver table had been set up in the back of the room. It was overladen with food that steamed as she watched, although she was certain the fruit and bowls of porridge would already be cold once she tried to eat them.

The Goblin Queen sat at the center of the table. She'd changed her icy crown for one that was more demure. A small tiara was set in the intricate curls of her hair, dusted with diamonds so bright they looked like the sun. Her gown was so delicately made that Freya wondered if it was frozen droplets of ice on a spiderweb. The long bell sleeves complimented her thin frame, and the wide neck revealed lovely shoulders and a long, swan-like neck.

The Queen lifted one of her manicured fingers and crooked it. She beckoned Freya forward as though she were nothing more than a little girl for her to play with. A toy or a doll, perhaps.

And yet, Freya went as soon as she was beckoned. Who was she to argue with the Queen of this place? She didn't want to end up like the faerie who had shattered on the floor.

Freya was acutely aware of her messy hair, rumpled clothing, and likely sleep lined face. At least there was no one else in the room to see just how horrible she looked, but the Queen seemed like the type who would care about that sort of thing. At least the Goblin King hadn't minded if she was muddy from her adventures. He'd still thought she was equally terrifying because of her wit.

"How did you sleep?" The Goblin Queen asked, gesturing for Freya to take a seat.

"Well," Freya lied through her teeth. "It was perhaps a little cold for my liking, but the room is exquisite."

"I thought you'd think so." With a flourish, the Queen gestured to all the food. How she didn't get her sleeve in the porridge, Freya would never know. "Eat, mortal. It is my understanding your kind needs much of this."

Freya reached for a bowl of porridge and dragged it closer. She tried to put a spoon in it, but the metal clicked against the frozen oats. Licking her lips, she looked to the next item and grabbed a bunch of grapes.

At least if these were frozen, she could still eat them.

"Thank you," she replied. "Why did you want to eat breakfast with me?"

The Queen lifted her hands and clapped them. The thunderous sound rocked through the room, and the icy waterfall cracked open, spilling out twenty women. Each wearing a gossamer gown puffed around their waists. They walked on their toes, like ballerinas, their bare feet silent as they padded over the floor. Ribbons swirled around their wrists and floated in the air as they moved.

Patterns of white snowflakes were stuck to their cheeks. Or perhaps, as Freya leaned closer to peer at the women, they were scarred onto their cheeks.

She realized they were. Scars in all shapes and sizes, but all snowflakes on each dancer's face.

Horrified, she tried not to let that show as the women lifted their arms over their heads and began to dance.

"Do you like the entertainment?" The Queen asked. "I've always found watching them was far more entertaining than music. Don't you think?"

No, she didn't think that at all. Watching these women silently dance, as though they couldn't make any sound at all, was eerie. Strange. It made her heart hurt because she wondered where these women had come from and why they were here, of all places.

But she couldn't say that. Instead, she had to swallow her fear and smile. "They're lovely. Where did you find such perfect specimens?"

"Would it surprise you to know they're from all over my kingdom?" The Queen watched them with rapt attention, as though she couldn't take her eyes off their movements. "Each more lovely than the last. I spent a very long time, when I was young, finding the perfect women for my dancers."

Freya didn't want to think about their families. The lives these women had left behind were just as important as their queen's entertainment.

She reached for a goblet that hopefully still had liquid in it. Tilting it back, she was relieved when coffee hit her tongue. It was icy, and the top had a thick film on it, but this was still coffee. It would at least steel her resolve.

Setting the goblet down, she nodded. "You have impressive tastes."

"Far better than my predecessor." The Goblin Queen lounged in her chair, the position very similar to the Goblin King's limp posture. "Why don't you tell me how you defeated him again? I'd like to hear the story in more detail."

Finally, something Freya could tell without fearing that she'd step into her own lies. She saw no reason she shouldn't tell the Goblin Queen everything that happened. The items were in her possession still, and even then she didn't think they were all that useful. The Goblin King had made up tasks that were inconsequential.

Freya told the story until her voice went hoarse. She spared no detail in the hopes that she would win the Goblin Queen over. After all, that was the plan. Make the Goblin Queen trust her, and then maybe something would slip about Eldridge.

It wasn't a brilliant plan, in hindsight.

When she finished, the Queen smiled at her with too much happiness in her expression. "So you really did defeat him. Well and truly, although you had some help along the way."

"I couldn't have done it without my companion," Freya corrected. "The goblin was exceedingly useful."

"Goblins have a way of seeming more helpful than they actually are." The Queen tapped a finger to her chin. "I'm surprised your people even allowed you to come here. Mortals hate magic, as they should. You're all rather careless with your powers. Like a child beating a drum whenever it wants attention."

Did she know?

Freya felt her stomach drop to her feet at the thought. If the Queen realized that Freya had cast a spell in her room, maybe she would start to suspect her actions weren't genuine. What would happen if the Queen thought Freya was here for other reasons?

Clearing her throat, Freya opened her mouth to plead for forgiveness.

She didn't get the chance.

"No matter, I suppose. You wouldn't be so foolish as to use magic in this castle. I'd know." The Queen gestured to her dancers. "And I enjoy having you around, my dear. I can't wait to hear more stories from your adventures. There is nothing I relish more in this life than hearing about the Goblin King losing."

"I have many more stories to tell," she replied.

"Good. Then I plan on seeing you as often as I can. You'll become one of my new dancers, just with storytelling. How lovely to have met you!" The Goblin Queen giggled. "I think I'll keep you for quite some time. But for now, admire my beautiful snowflakes with me."

Freya was glad for the opportunity to no longer look at the Goblin Queen. She took another deep swallow of coffee and then stared at the young women dancing.

If she could keep the Goblin Queen on her side, then surely the woman would say something. Eventually. She had to know where the Goblin King was being kept, and if Freya became her dear friend, then the Queen would let the truth slip. All Freya had to do was last that long.

Her eyes fell on the dancing women once again. Their hair never moved as they spun across the dance floor. Their skirts swirled in graceful arcs around them, and their arms spun with elegant grace. She'd never seen dancers who moved with such perfection.

Then she looked at the floor.

Blood smeared the ice where their feet scraped the rough ice. Every step stuck their heated toes to the cold floor. To move, they had to rip the skin to take another step. Each movement pulled and broke at the poor dancer's bodies.

And yet, they still danced. They moved with purpose and

didn't even flinch when their skin peeled off and revealed the muscle and bone beneath. They kept moving. Whether that was with fear or delusion, she would never know.

Freya's heart raced. She took a deep, shuddering breath and another swift swallow of coffee. She wished it was wine. Or rum.

Something strong enough to get her through this breakfast and whatever the coming months would bring. This place was more than just an ice castle. The entire mountain was a prison, made to horrify and control.

All she could hope was that she didn't end up like these dancers. Broken. Bleeding. Playing to the whims of their dangerous queen.

Freya returned to her room with a heavy heart after watching the dancer's nearly destroy themselves for the Queen. None of them had even complained or winced when they finally stopped. They just smiled at their ruler, dropped into curtsies, and then returned into the waterfall where they disappeared from sight.

Freya couldn't have done that. They must have been sturdy women to not show any reaction or response to tearing their feet up like that.

She stepped into her room after following the ice creature once more. Something else had been bothering her since the moment she realized the dancers were little more than slaves. This creature whom the Queen had made... Was it more alive than she thought?

She turned around as it left and asked, "Is there anything I can call you?"

The creature's eyes rolled in the ice of its head. "Why?"

"Everything has a name."

It pondered the question for a bit before finally replying, "No. I don't have a name."

The little thing toddled off again with its high heels tapping on the ice. She resolved herself to figuring out a name it might like, because she refused to believe it didn't want one. Or maybe because it was made entirely by the Queen's magic. The thought of a name was an idea it couldn't comprehend.

She closed the door and scolded herself. "Freya, you're getting too involved already. Just keep pushing forward, the Queen will eventually give you something to work with."

"Really?" Arrow crawled out from under the ice bed and shook himself. "I don't think she'll admit to a single thing. The Goblin Queen is smarter than we gave her credit for."

"Arrow!" The name burst out of her mouth. Freya lunged forward and scooped the goblin into her arms. "You have no idea how worried I was. Where have you been? Did they make you dance on ice?"

He wriggled in her arms, frantically trying to pull himself from her grip. "I have no idea what you're talking about, you ridiculous woman. Unhand me!"

Freya gave him one last squeeze before dropping him back onto the ground.

He reared up on his back legs and tugged hard on his woolen jacket, forcing it back into place. "You've rumpled my clothes again. Do you know how hard it was to press them without an iron?"

"I can imagine it was rather difficult, I apologize for worrying that the Queen might have killed you." She crossed her arms firmly over her chest. "What are you doing here, anyway?"

"I thought you would have figured something out by now. Obviously I was wrong." He huffed out a breath and walked toward the fireplace. "They didn't even give you a fire?"

"No, I have figured nothing out. Sorry to disappoint." Freya reached out and dusted snow off the top of the mantle. "It was warm in here last night, I swear. I don't know how, but there was a fire and the Goblin King."

"Eldridge visited again?" Arrow grumbled. "He's got to stop doing that. That man will use up all his magic just to keep in touch, when he knows he can't tell us where he is. He's going to hurt himself."

"You think? Or he's going to hurt me." She touched a hand to her head. "I've been getting splitting headaches for a while, ever since he disappeared. I thought it was because of the magic in this realm, but then I realized I've been getting them before he appears."

"So he's wriggling into your head then." Arrow snorted. His ears flopped dramatically on either side of his head. "He knows better than to pry into the mind of a mortal. He could get lost in your head and then we'd all really be in trouble."

"Do I want to know why?" Freya wasn't sure that she did. The more she heard about magic, the more curious she was. And then where would she be?

She was still a mortal. Even the Queen claimed that mortals making magic were clunky at best, and she didn't want to conjure a spell that might go wrong.

Arrow shook his head. "Mortal minds aren't like the fae. We keep everything in nice, neat little compartments in our minds. It's why we sometimes appear emotionless to your kind. But mortal heads? They're labyrinths that are sometimes impossible to get out of. If he's altering the reality you see, that can be even more dangerous. He needs to preserve his strength. Faeries realms, who knows what the Goblin Queen is doing to him."

She had a bit of an idea. Considering how lank and thin Eldridge was looking in her visions of him, she thought it safe to assume the Queen was not treating the previous king to afternoon tea.

Clearing her throat, she turned her attention back to the frozen fireplace. "I've been entirely unsuccessful in finding out anything new. The Queen is keeping me close, but all she wants is to hear how I beat the Goblin King."

"She'll make a mistake soon enough." Arrow's tail wagged, betraying what he was about to say long before he opened his mouth. "But I found something of interest. It's not where the King is, but it's close."

Freya's heart leapt in her chest. He was closer to finding the Goblin King? "Why didn't you say something sooner?"

Arrow shrugged. "Dramatic effect. Come on."

Together they left her room and snuck down the hall. She followed her goblin dog with pure faith that he knew where he was going, because she certainly didn't. Every hallway looked the same. There were no doors. No windows. No differences to keep track of.

Just blue ice tunnels that stretched so far into the distance they disappeared into deep cobalt.

"Where are we going?" she whispered. "Won't someone see us?"

Arrow shook his head, dropping onto all fours to speed up. "Not unless there is a servant wandering around. I don't think there's many people in this castle, Freya."

"Why's that?"

He looked over his shoulder, gaze haunted with memories. "I don't think she's woken most of the Winter Court up yet."

Well, that was even more ominous. Why would the Queen keep her own court asleep when she could wake them? Curiouser and curiouser.

Arrow finally stopped. The wall in front of them was chipped at the bottom, and she could see the faint outline of scratch marks. Deep furrows that looked quite a bit like a dog had been trying to dig underneath the wall.

"How did you know something was there?" she asked.

"I could smell it."

Impressive. She always forgot he could use his nose like a real dog.

Freya leaned down and wiggled her fingers into the gap he'd scratched. The ice was sharper than knives. It didn't take long for her own blood to tinge the icy crystals a bright red. But she managed to get her hands underneath enough to wiggle the door open.

The ice slid forward with a groan, giving enough room for them to slip inside the hidden room. She glanced over her shoulder to make sure no one was watching them and then ducked inside.

Arrow murmured, "Close the door. There's usually guards in front of this, but I made a mess in the kitchen. The servants were screaming when I left. Should take a while for the guards to clean up that whole mess."

"Guards?" she hissed, but went back to work, tugging the door closed. Her fingers screamed with pain. "You said no one was in the halls?"

"And there was no one in the halls when we first got here. None of my words were a lie." He flicked his tail straight up into the air and then started down the long, narrow room. The white tip of his tail waved like a flag. "You'll forgive me once you see what I've found."

Freya huffed out an angry breath and finished tugging the door closed. She hoped they could leave when they were finished here. The door sure seemed stuck. Standing, she dusted her hands off on her now worn jacket and spun.

The room was yet another icy construction. All the walls were a pale color, though. Almost transparent, with small white bubbles of air pockets. There was no furniture, no decorations, nothing that would make this room look like anyone used it at all. The dim light barely even lit up the space for her to see what surrounded them.

"What is this place?" she asked, walking up to Arrow with a frown.

"Step closer to the ice," he replied. His voice was an indistinct murmur of horror. "See for yourself."

She stepped up to the ice and then suddenly the room filled with light. As if someone had spelled it for the moment when another person would step close to the wall. And in front of her was a man who met her gaze with a look of horror in his own. A mortal man, it seemed, although he would never move again.

Freya gasped and retreated from the wall, but the distance only revealed a harsher truth. The soft, golden light illuminated a hundred bodies all hidden within the ice. Frozen in blocks. Still standing at attention as though they could step out of the wall at any time. They were stuck in a single moment with their clothing perfectly preserved and fear still etched on their expressions.

Her hands shook. Freya lifted one to press against her mouth, emotions boiling in her chest. She wanted to rage at the Goblin Queen for taking so many lives. She wanted to scream at the woman who could cause so much hurt and not feel guilt for her choices.

But all Freya could do was shiver in fear. The power it must have taken to suspend all these people's lives... It was unfathomable.

"Who are they?" she asked.

"These are some people from the Winter Court," Arrow replied. "Some of them are merely playthings the Goblin Queen found interesting before she took the throne. They've all been in there for a very long time, I would guess."

Pity made her stomach roll around and her breakfast press against her throat. If she stared for any longer, then she would vomit all over the floor and then someone would know she and Arrow had been here.

A single word played in her mind. *Prison.* They were searching for a prison.

This was obviously a kind of jail, and that meant the Goblin King might be here. Where else would the Goblin Queen have hidden him in this icy castle?

Freya bolted into motion, pressing a single finger against the ice and moving down the line as quickly as she could. "Not him," she whispered over and over until she reached the end of the room. Then, she spun around and did it on the other side.

Arrow let her try to find the Goblin King. He had probably done the same thing when he first found this room, but she had to check. She had to see for herself that they were still going to be in this hellish place because they hadn't found him. Not this easily.

She stopped beside Arrow and pressed both hands to the ice in front of him. This woman was frozen in a beautiful white gown that looked like a wedding dress. She was one of the few who weren't standing. Instead, this lovely dark haired woman was curled up on her side as though she was asleep.

The Goblin Queen had likely trapped this pretty girl in the castle, and then she just never woke up.

Perhaps that would happen to Freya, too.

Her head split open like someone had struck it with a hatchet. Wincing, she pressed her hand to her forehead. The scent of apple pie bloomed in her nose long before she heard the caramel tones of his voice.

"Did you think it would be so easy?" Eldridge asked. "She won't keep me in a place where anyone could find me."

Arrow hissed out a long breath. "My king." The dog bent down until his chin touched the floor. "You're alive."

The Goblin King's reflection stood just beside the sleeping bride. He met Freya's gaze with one of sadness and complete disappointment. "You aren't looking for me hard enough, Freya."

"What would you have me do?" she whispered. "Tear the castle apart with an army of creatures half man, half beast? I could do that. I could get all your old court and force them into another war. Another faerie war that would tear apart the courts and then you could put the pieces back together again."

"Another war?" He shook his head. "No, I don't want that. You know I don't want that."

She remembered the journal, the one he did not know she had read. His diary was nothing more than frantic scribbles and moments of memory from a war that had torn apart his people and his land. But she remembered the emotion in his handwriting. The pain he had felt in knowing that all the creatures were fighting and there was nothing he could do to stop their hatred.

Freya lifted her hand and pressed it against the ice that stood between them. "We're looking for you, Eldridge. I just need something more to work with. If you can't tell me where you are, then tell me something about the Goblin Queen that I can use against her. Something that will convince her to trust me."

He lifted his hand to mirror hers. She could almost feel him through the ice. The warmth of his touch and the magic that came with it. "She hates me, Freya. That's all the clue you need. Fuel that hatred and give her the impression that you hate me as well. Then she will trust you and tell you anything you desire."

She smiled softly. "It shouldn't be too hard to pretend that, now, should it? I do hate you, after all. You're the villain in my story."

"And you're the hero in mine," he whispered. Eldridge flexed his fingers on the ice, as though he desperately wanted to touch her and resented that he couldn't reach through the glass.

His image faded away, and she was left standing alone with Arrow once again.

She took a deep breath. Nodded. Then looked at Arrow with determination. "We're going to find him. We just need to figure out how."

CHAPTER 11

A few days came and went before the little monster showed up at her door again. Freya passed the time by pressing her hands together, breathing into her fingers, and pacing. She knew exactly how many steps it took to get from one end to the other of her room. No amount of pacing helped the anxiety in her chest, however.

They were running out of time. The Goblin King hadn't reached out to her at all since they had stood in that frozen prison with all the Goblin Queen's remaining court. The ones she refused to wake up.

Why?

Why wouldn't the Queen wake up the people who were supposed to be her own? Surely they would be willing and able to help her. They would want to give her more power with this newly acquired throne.

Unless they were the ones who would force her to leave the Winter Court. After all, a Goblin Queen couldn't stay the queen of her own court. Maybe this terrifying woman didn't want to give up her birthright, knew her own people would force her out.

Freya had too many questions, and she knew none of them would get answered without becoming friends with the Queen.

She followed the ice creature through the halls and into an area that split open to the sky. Freya stared up in shock at the sight of the sun. Had they traveled higher in the mountain? She hadn't felt like her legs were working harder. Every hallway seemed entirely flat. But this fissure in the ground had split to the sky. Though the walls were far too high for her to climb.

This wasn't an opportunity for an escape. It was still the same confinement that she'd always been in.

Sighing, she stared straight ahead at what looked like a massive greenhouse. Except, the glass walls were ice that warped her view of what was inside. Other than a single dark figure who stood in the center.

The creature pointed toward the shadow. "The Queen would like to speak with you."

Freya nodded, then looked down at the creature with a small smile on her face. "I think I'm going to call you Frost, if that's all right with you."

Frost blinked up at her and then seemed to frown. "Why would you call me that?"

"Because everyone needs a name." Without thinking, she touched a hand to the creature's head. "Even you, though you seem to think you don't want one. I promise, a name makes you more of a person than just something animated by magic. A name has meaning."

The ice creature touched a hand to its chest as she walked away. Freya heard the smallest whisper as it repeated the name.

"Frost. My name is Frost." The sound of icy high heels clicking over the ground followed the words.

Good. At least now the icy creature might be on her side too.

Freya walked all the way into the greenhouse with its two story high ice walls and gaped at the beauty inside. At least there were no snow drifts here. The floors were a blue marble, not ice, and there were white columns creating a second level. If this had been any other greenhouse, there might have been ivy tangled over the columns and growing in the sun. But even in this room the air was cold. Her breath puffed before her.

There were plants here though, or at least fake ones. Icy roses grew in every corner, and small trees that were carved out of snow. The Goblin Queen had created the semblance of a greenhouse in this place. But it was still cold and vacant of life.

The Queen stood in the center with her white blonde hair spilling down her back. Her gown today was made of midnight blue, deep and rich in color. It hugged tight to her form, revealing that she was a stunning creature beneath all that fabric. Too beautiful for words.

"Ah, Esther," the Goblin Queen said. "I'm glad you could join me. I was starting to think that you had told my guard that you wouldn't see me."

Esther?

Ah, right. She had lied about her name. Damn it, she was already forgetting her own rules.

Clearing her throat, Freya chuckled and strode up to the Queen's side. "And if I had refused to see you?"

The Queen's gaze shifted, a fire burning in them that was hotter than a regular flame. Blue and white hot. "Then I would have made you, of course. You're in my court for one reason, and one reason alone. My entertainment."

Yes, it seemed like everyone in this court was only here to ensure their Queen was enjoying herself. But that wasn't the way to rule, even Freya knew that.

She took a deep breath and decided to change the subject. This was already going in a direction she didn't want. The Queen needed to be happy, and the Goblin King had said the only way to do that was to talk to her about hating him.

Freya could do that. She could pretend to hate the King. All she had to do was remember how she had felt the first time she had seen him.

Easy.

Walking away from the Queen, she approached the roses and

bent down to stare at their delicate construction. "You know, the Goblin King would have hated these. At least, that was my impression of him."

The Queen hesitated for a few moments, then she walked up to Freya's side. "Yes, he would have. Your impression is correct."

"Why do you think he would hate them?" She tilted her head to the side, staring even closer at the roses that were so delicate they almost looked like they were alive. "They're beautiful."

"And delicate. The Goblin King hates anything that's fragile like this. He wants every plant, animal, and person to be strong enough to care for themselves." The Goblin Queen reached out and cupped the nearest rose, then crushed it in her fist. "If something can be ruined so easily, then he thinks it has no place in our world."

Freya now understood why Eldridge was so fascinated with mortals, and perhaps even in Freya herself. It made sense that he would want powerful things to surround him. Stronger than the normal mortal, and certainly a peasant woman would be that. Freya knew how to take care of herself and her sister. But more so, she wasn't a delicate faerie who expected things to be handed to her. She worked for what she had, sometimes struggling for years to get it.

She straightened, trying hard not to stare at the shattered pieces of the rose on the floor. So similar to the pieces of the faerie the Queen had crushed. "And you hate him as much as he hates these roses. Don't you?"

The Queen met her gaze with a small smile that showed her pleasure in the topic. "Oh yes, I hate him more than anything in this realm. And he deserves that hatred. Don't you agree?"

The lie burned on her tongue. "Yes. Most likely. He's a dangerous man who takes what he wants."

"That's why I like you, Esther. I think you understand why I hate him." The Queen reached forward and touched a fingernail underneath Freya's chin. The bitter touch burned. "Tell me why you loathe the monster."

She tried to push all the anger she'd felt at him in that memory into her gaze. Freya forced herself to relive that moment when she had realized the goblins had stolen her sister. "Because he kidnapped my sister for taking a necklace that looked like our mother's. She didn't buy it from the goblin market, she just wanted to see if it was the same one our mother wore. That was all. And then when I realized she had disappeared, I knew I had to beat him and get her back."

The Queen stroked the nail along Freya's jaw, her gaze wide with rapture. "Such passion. You truly think him a beast."

"I told him he was the villain in my story." Freya swallowed hard. "And if I saw him again, I would tell him the same thing. He's still the villain. A demon."

That was the truth, although the anger with the words had dulled. She didn't think he was really a monster anymore. There were layers to his person that she had yet to uncover, and that she was interested to learn.

The Goblin Queen dropped her hand and sighed. Even that movement was pretty and delicate. "You know I used to think of him as my brother?"

"Really?" Freya backed away from the Queen, but then sat on a nearby bench. Hopefully the movement would look like she wanted to rest rather than create space between herself and the horrible queen. "A brother? I thought he was born in the Autumn Court?"

"He was. But his family didn't like him very much, you see. The feeling about Eldridge runs in all the veins of the fae. No one liked him. My family took him in as pity, hoping that he would grow into someone we could love." She lifted her hand and a tiny figure of Eldridge appeared in her palm.

He was young in the swirling snowflakes that created him. His shoulders were held a little straighter and his hip was cocked at a sharper angle. He obviously thought highly of himself. Perhaps that was the posture of a faerie soldier, she didn't know.

Freya's heart leapt into her throat at the sight of him. *Don't react,* she told herself. *Stay angry and don't let her see all the complicated emotions that are swirling in your chest.*

She licked her lips and pointed at the figure. "How strange to think that he would have sought help from the Winter Court. In my experience, none of the faeries of any court like each other."

"We don't. But the Winter Court was more giving in those days." The Queen crushed the figure in her hand as she had the rose. "He used to tell me I was capable of great things and great kindness."

Freya shouldn't have pried even further. She didn't want to know the answer, but some part of her screamed to ask the question. And so she did. "Are you?"

The Goblin Queen's blue eyes lit up with an inner light, glowing with power. "Capable of great things? Yes. Capable of great kindness? No."

Freya's stomach twisted, and she felt nothing but fear once again. None of the other faerie leaders had made her so afraid other than this icy woman who didn't see mercy in the world. The Goblin Queen would stomp upon anyone who stood in her way, and Freya didn't think she would feel bad about it.

This Queen would kill and slaughter and destroy. She desired to see the world at her feet and then to laugh in its face.

Tucking her shaking hands into her skirts, Freya tried to change the conversation yet again. "My Queen, I have a question for you. It's my hope that you have seen worth and value in my presence in your castle."

"Oh, indeed. You are quite entertaining, my dear. I have never been more interested in a mortal, and that's a compliment."

It didn't feel like a compliment. Actually, it felt like a threat.

Freya tried very hard to not let the words bother her. She would survive this, just as she had survived so much more. "If you didn't notice, I'm still in the same clothing I was in when I arrived. My hope is that you may have some great kindness still within you to dress me in something other than an old woolen coat and underthings that have seen quite a few days of travel and freezing."

The Queen looked her up and down, then her eyes seemed to clear. Her mouth curved into a wicked smile. "Oh, my dear. I'm so sorry that I haven't noticed your... predicament. Yes, of course I will clothe you. I have so many things that are leftovers from the old Winter Court, and I think I would very much enjoy seeing what you look like with them on. A mortal, wearing the garb of the Winter Palace."

Was this a good thing? Freya didn't know. This could be a massive mistake to ask the queen to invest even more time in her, but Freya was just starting to hear the story of the Goblin King from this new Queen's lips.

So she would do whatever the woman wanted.

Freya flinched when the Goblin Queen clapped her hands.

"Come, mortal!" she shouted. "Let's see what you look like in clothing made for royalty."

CHAPTER 12

Freya followed the Goblin Queen through a small back door in the greenhouse and then through the winding halls yet again. She was so tired of looking at blue ice. Freya desired to see bright green grass and a splash of pink and red in the sky. Any color. Anything other than damned blue.

The Queen led her all the way into a room that functioned as a sort of closet. The closets appeared to be more tunnels that hid so much fabric it made Freya's head spin. Was this where all the ladies of the court would get dressed? Why wouldn't they have these dresses in their own rooms?

The Goblin Queen lifted her arms. Blue magic spilled in glittering sparkles from her hands and down her arms. It landed on the ground and funneled toward the walls. Deep blue glowed from within the ice, and then ten of the ice creatures stepped out.

They were all slightly different. Their eyes were shaped in round circles or squeezed ovals. Some of them had pointed feet, while others were flat nubs at the end. But they weren't the ice creature she was used to.

"Hello," Freya said.

"You're so polite," the Goblin Queen laughed. "They don't know how to talk. Not like the one I send to go get you. Apparently talking made bringing you to my side easier. It's gotten rather annoying with all those words, though. Would you like a new one?"

That sounded like the Queen would kill the ice creature if Freya was disappointed with it. And she wasn't. She'd just named the poor thing!

"No!" she almost shouted the word. Clearing her throat, she shook her head to emphasize the word. "That one suits me just fine."

"Really, I can make any of them do whatever you want. If that one doesn't look the way you desire, then I can just make another one." The Goblin Queen waved at the ice creatures that approached Freya. "They're much easier than real servants. They don't need food or attention. They just need to know what their job is and they go about it. You see? Already they want to help you out of your clothing. Now, let me pick out the perfect dress for you."

The Goblin Queen turned around and marched toward the closets like she was going to war. And maybe this was her kind of war, Freya didn't know.

Freya thought it was probably not smart to argue with the ice creatures that already had their tiny hands outstretched. If they were going to help her, then so be it.

She lifted her arms and let the monsters go to work. Their icy hands dragged down her body, and she hated every second of their cold strokes. It was like dead things were pulling her clothing off.

A splitting headache preceded Eldridge's voice in her ear. "This is different from the last time a faerie dressed you, now isn't it?"

She couldn't reply to him, damn it. He had to know the Goblin Queen was right in front of her, and obviously she wouldn't be talking to the ice creatures. One of them had stepped on top of another to pull her jacket down over her back and now was working on the laces of her woolen gown.

"What are you doing?" she whispered under her breath.

"Entertaining myself," he replied. The Goblin King stepped in front of her, arms crossed over his chest and head tilted to the side. "Isn't that what Goblin Kings are supposed to do? That's what she was telling you, at least."

Freya gritted her teeth and glared at him. This was too much of a risk. The Goblin Queen could turn around at any point and see him standing there.

"Esther?" the Queen called out. "What color looks good on your skin, my dear?"

She shook her head, breath coming ragged out of her lips. "I don't know."

"You don't know?" The Queen turned around and Freya knew that this was the moment when it all crumbled down. The damned Goblin King had ruined everything once again, sabotaging himself so he'd have to stay here forever in her clutches.

Eldridge remained standing in front of her, watching as the ice creatures undressed her. And the Queen continued to stare at her with a look of impatience.

She couldn't see Eldridge, Freya realized. The Queen couldn't see the Goblin King because, for her, he wasn't really there.

"Esther," the Queen snapped.

"Yes?" Freya whispered the word, too quiet but completely unsure what the question was. Everything in her head was racing, afraid of what the Queen would find out and if she could hide it fast enough.

"You know, if I didn't know better, I would think that wasn't your name at all." The Queen shook her head, then turned back to the clothing. "You never respond as quickly as I want. Get your head out of worrying about what my servants are doing and focus on becoming a more beautiful version of yourself. Pick a color, my dear."

She couldn't pick a color when all this was going on. Freya didn't care what color the Queen picked.

Eldridge watched her with an amused grin. "Yes, Freya. What color do you want to wear? You always look so fetching in blue."

She wasn't playing this game with the two of them watching her like a hawk. "White," she stuttered. "Isn't that the color of your kingdom? White as snow, my Queen. That would be the color I would be most honored to wear."

The Queen clucked, then moved deeper into the closet until she disappeared from sight. "What a color to pick! White. I wouldn't have thought with your pale skin that color would look good on you, but if you insist. It's only going to make you look more pale and drawn, you know."

Then pick a different color, Freya wanted to scream. She didn't care!

The ice creatures finished unlacing her dress. They pushed it over her shoulders until the fabric slumped to the ground. She was left in only her underthings while they gathered up all her old clothes and dragged them away.

Freya wrapped an arm around her chest and used the other hand to hide herself from the Goblin King's gaze. At least no one was looking at her so she could hiss, "Would you turn around?"

"I don't think so," he replied, that stupid grin still on his face. "You're far too lovely, my dear. Would you look at all that pale skin?"

"I'd prefer it if you didn't."

"Oh no, this is a perfect opportunity for me to make you uncomfortable. And I'm enjoying myself." He took a step closer, leaning down to look at her hip. "Where did you get this scar? I must know the story."

She couldn't flinch away fast enough. The Goblin Queen came out of the closet with a massive white gown in her arms. "Will this do? I don't know how warm you have to be."

Freya looked up, panicked. The dress was ugly as sin, but it would do. It didn't matter to her if the dress would make her look like her great aunt. Put it on her and hide her skin. "Yes, that's lovely."

The Queen frowned and threw the dress onto the ground. "That was a test! This dress is ugly, and you'd look awful in it. Really, girl, do you not have any sense of fashion?"

"Wait—" Freya tried to stop the Queen from returning into the closet, but she already disappeared beyond the dresses.

Huffing out an angry breath, she pursed her lips and looked back at the Goblin King. "Eldridge, stop looking at me."

He straightened, eyes glazed and a stupid smile on his face. "Why would I ever do that? You're a beautiful woman, Freya. I didn't know how much more lovely you could get until this moment. I mean really, look at you! You're like a rose ready to be plucked."

"What kind of nonsense is that? Snap out of it, you idiot."

He leaned forward, almost touching his nose to her hair. "Really, I'm not lying. You know I cannot lie. I find you completely irresistible."

"I'm going to slap you." She needed to focus, and he was distracting her worse than normal.

"You wouldn't dare."

She whipped her arm back and struck out like a snake snapping at a mouse. Her hand clapped across his face and the sound echoed far too loudly. Eldridge flinched back with a sound of shock, pressing his hand against his bright red cheek.

"What was that for?" he whined.

"Be better," she snarled.

The Queen came out at the same second, holding another gown that was far more beautiful. The neckline was a modest square, while the skirts flared out only a little at the hips. It would be warm and still give her enough space to move. "Did I hear you strike something?"

Freya struggled to figure out what would make sense. Finally she shrugged and said, "I thought I felt a spider on my leg. I slapped at it, but there was nothing there. Must have just been a phantom feeling."

The Queen strode to her side and held the dress out. "You must tell me if you ever find a spider in my castle, my dear. I hate the dreadful things and have no place for them in the Winter Court. It's why I keep it so cold."

Freya had an idea it was for more reasons than that. Sighing, she took the dress and nodded. "Of course, my Queen."

The ice creatures stacked themselves beside her again, reaching out for the gown with their tiny hands. Freya gave the dress away and let herself be stuffed into the fabric.

The whole time, Eldridge stood behind the Goblin Queen. If looks killed, he would have seared through the Goblin Queen's flesh. Though he wasn't as intimidating as normal. Rubbing his bright red cheek made him look a little... well. Adorable.

Freya held herself still until the ice creatures finished with their work. One of them hopped down, moved to stand by the Queen, and then put its tiny ice hands on its hips. Together, the creature and the Queen looked her up and down until the Queen finally nodded.

"Yes, that will do. Now you look far less like a mortal who stumbled into my castle from the forest. You really were looking like something the Summer Lord would have enjoyed. Too..." The Goblin Queen waggled her fingers in the air. "Earthy."

Eldridge curled his lip in disgust. "You wouldn't know something that looked earthy if it hit you in the face, Lumi. All you see is a beautiful woman who might actually hold a candle to your own beauty."

Was she supposed to respond? Freya furrowed her brows in concentration and forced a smile. "Thank you. I feel more at home here now that I'm wearing something more appropriate."

At least she had sleeves. Now all she had to do was find another jacket that would cover her up, and she'd look more like she belonged here. And the more she looked like she belonged, the more the Queen would like her.

"Yes, before you looked too much like someone, the Goblin King would like. And you know how much we want to avoid that." The Queen reached her hand out for the ice creature to take. "My little servant, would you please go get the fur coat? You know the one."

The creature walked right through Eldridge as though he weren't even there. Or perhaps as though he were a ghost.

She supposed he sort of was in this form.

Freya took a deep breath and tried to think of something else to say. Something that would prove she wasn't distracted. "I'm curious what the Goblin King's type was, then. If he would prefer earthy things, then how did he end up in the Winter Court?"

The Queen's gaze flashed in anger. "Because he enjoys being disappointed, of course. Eldridge never wanted anyone to love him. He wanted to be worshipped, revered, and perhaps even feared. But he never knew what love was, and he wouldn't have recognized it if it had bitten him in the ass."

With a sudden lunging movement, Eldridge put himself in front of the Queen's face and snarled, "You raging bitch. You know damned well that's a lie, and yet those poisonous words can still drip from your tongue?"

Freya wanted to shout at him to stop. She couldn't focus on what the Queen was saying when he was screaming in her face as though he were already standing in the room.

A little whine escaped her lips before she licked them and replied, "That sounds like a horrible way to live. Perhaps you should have pitied him."

"Ah, yes." The Queen smiled and tilted her head back as though rays of sunlight were playing on her face. "Pity for the Goblin King. That sounds like a wonderful idea."

If he could have ripped out the Queen's throat, he likely would have. Rage turned his features into something dangerous and fearsome. Yet, Freya had to keep up this charade that she hated him, when all she wanted to do was save him. To get

Eldridge away from this monstrous woman who wanted to harm him and everything he loved.

Blowing out a long, steadying breath, she forced herself to smile and spin in a circle. "Well, my Queen? Are you happy with your work? You've turned this country peasant into a real noble of the Winter Court!"

"Maybe not a noble," the Queen replied, but the smile on her face said otherwise. "But you are certainly easier to look at now, my dear. You could sit at my table and you wouldn't embarrass me."

Freya nearly tumbled forward she moved so quickly. She intercepted the ice creature holding the white fur jacket, snagging it and flipping it over her shoulders with a flourish. She spun in one more circle before winking at the Queen. "Then why don't we go on an adventure, my Queen? Just you and I."

"What adventure would you like?"

"Oh, I don't know." She tried to infuse her voice with excitement, when all she felt was nauseous. "Show me everything. I find myself enchanted by your kingdom, Goblin Queen."

Those were the magic words, apparently.

The Queen straightened, puffing out her chest with pride before holding out her arm for Freya to take. "Then let me show you my world, Esther."

CHAPTER 13

Freya paced back and forth beside her bed. Another week had passed, and she'd gotten nowhere. The Queen had shown her all over the castle and she was no closer to finding Eldridge.

This place was a labyrinth. Larger than the one in front of the Summer Lord's castle. Freya was certain she could spend an entire lifetime trying to figure out this maze, and it would still change before she finished walking through the entirety.

"The Queen makes the hallways realign themselves every few days," she told Arrow. "She changes them so that no one can know how to get from point A to point B without walking through the ice itself."

He stretched on the bed where she had laid out the blankets and furs for him to be more comfortable. "Then we break through the walls."

She shook her head. "They are thick. Too thick, really. It would take me a few hours to break through one, and then she would have already felt the difference in her building. Her magic runs through everything."

"It can't run through everything," he grumbled. "Even the Goblin King wasn't that powerful."

Freya rubbed her eyes, trying to think through the exhaustion. She'd been trying so hard to entertain the Goblin Queen that she really hadn't had time for herself. Sleeping wasn't an option when the Queen had a new plaything.

"Then she's getting her power from somewhere else," she muttered. "Or something else."

A new voice interrupted them. "Could it be that she's getting her power from someone else?"

She let out a long, frustrated groan. "Of course you show up now. Where have you been?"

The Goblin King sat on the bed beside Arrow, although the goblin dog spared not a single glance for his king. If anything, it appeared Arrow couldn't even see Eldridge.

Arrow lifted his head, perked up his ears, and searched the room for his king. Loyalty ran in his veins, strong and true. He would do anything for his king. No matter how difficult that task might be. "Is the king here?"

"You can't see him?" she asked.

When Arrow shook his head, she narrowed her gaze on Eldridge.

The Goblin King shrugged. "I'm only so powerful, Freya. Sometimes I can't let him see me. Sometimes I have to use you as a guide."

She rolled her eyes to the ceiling, frustrated with life at this point. "Eldridge says he doesn't have enough power for you to see him right now, Arrow. I don't have the faintest idea what that means, or why he would even say it, but here we are. I understand nothing in this realm is as it appears."

Eldridge leaned back on his hands. "Think about what I said first, Freya."

At the same time, Arrow replied, "Ask him what is wrong if he can't use his powers for both of us to see him, then."

She couldn't keep track of everyone in the room talking at the same time. They both needed to slow down because her head hurt so much it felt like it was going to explode.

Maybe Eldridge wasn't the only one getting weaker. The pain in between her eyes was making her shake. Lifting a hand, she pressed it against the side of her head and reminded herself to breathe. "He said that the Queen might be taking some of his power to add to her own. Something along those lines."

"Freya?"

She didn't know which one said her name. Her vision went blurry, and she staggered a few steps to the side. Why couldn't she balance?

Warm hands scooped underneath her arms. "Sit down before you fall down, Freya."

Eldridge lowered her onto his spot on the bed, sinking down onto his knees between her legs. His hands smoothed back and forth on her thighs, easing her through the dizzy spell and bringing the room back into focus.

Taking a deep breath, she inhaled through her nose and out through her mouth. Over and over until the room stopped spinning and she could actually see Eldridge on his knees.

"I'm sorry," she whispered. "I don't know what that was."

"A mixture of exhaustion and me using your mind a little too much." Eldridge reached up and smoothed a strand of her hair behind her ear. "Keep breathing, dear one. You will be fine, but you need to get your balance again. Your body needs to center itself."

"I don't know why it needs to, though." Her heart started racing again, and she couldn't quite catch her breath fast enough. "I just... I don't know what's happening at all anymore. I feel like I'm falling through my own life."

"No, no, Freya, you aren't falling." He shifted his hand to the back of her head and drew her down toward him. Pressing their foreheads together, he took a deep breath with her. "I won't let you fall. I have unlimited power, don't you know that? Magic that would pull the stars from the sky for you if you wished."

"But you're in a prison and I can't find you."

"I won't be there forever." He leaned back and grinned. His

thumbs stroked the high planes of her cheekbones. "You're the hero of this story, Freya. You're going to find me. Together, we will defeat the Goblin Queen and restore this world back to what it needs to be. You and I."

She liked the sound of that. At least then she wasn't alone anymore. It wasn't the weight of the entire world on her shoulders, pressing down until she was nothing more than a flattened soul underneath a mountain of responsibility.

Her lungs stopped screaming for breath. Her heart stopped racing. And it even seemed like the ache of the throbbing headache dulled ever so slightly.

She nodded. "All right. It's easier if this is together and not..."

"Apart?" he filled in the word for her.

"Yes."

Eldridge released her and stood back up. "We have never been apart, Freya. Ever since the first moment I saw you, I knew you wouldn't stray far from my soul."

What was she supposed to say to that? She was just a mortal woman, and she'd never even entertained a man at home. Yet this one could string together the most beautiful words she'd ever heard in her life.

A cold wet nose pressed against her arm. "Are you back to yourself yet?"

Of course. Arrow was in the room with them, and she couldn't stare at the Goblin King with moon eyes any longer.

Clearing her throat, she nodded. "Yes, Arrow. I'm so sorry to frighten you. Eldridge, I know it might be difficult, but could you show yourself to Arrow? Take whatever power from me you need. If that's even possible for you to take power from a mortal."

"I don't think you have any more to give," he muttered. "I will try my best."

Freya felt a tug deep in her belly, like he was pulling her spine through her stomach. She pressed a hand to her abdomen and winced, but didn't complain.

Eldridge's form shimmered. Whatever glamour he had put on himself disappeared with the action as well. One moment, he was the ragged looking king. Bruises appeared over his eye and jaw. A cut sliced through the top of his eyebrow and she didn't know if this was due to using the magic, or if he'd just been hiding the wounds from her.

Arrow growled, low and deep. "So she's taken to hurting you, then?"

"Just like old times," Eldridge replied. "There's no stopping her once she starts. You know how she loves to hear people scream."

Freya's heart broke in two. She had known he was in some kind of pain, but this?

"What is she doing to you?" she asked.

"I can't tell you that, Freya. This is just a distraction from what you need to do. You know that." He looked at her with so much hope in his gaze. Hope that she would be the one who finally made a difference. That she could save him even when she knew the likelihood of that was diminishing with every passing day.

She would do what she could. Freya could only move so fast and she hoped she would get to him in time.

Blinking past tears, she nodded. "Fine, then. You have to help us some, Eldridge. I cannot do this without your help. Together, remember?"

Arrow put his paw on her leg. "It's faerie law that no one can help the king, Freya. Not even himself. If he could tell us where he was, or give us any sort of hint, he would have by now."

"Damn the law," she snarled. "I don't care if the faeries say we're supposed to let him get strung up by his toes every night. Laws are meant to be broken."

"Not this one," Eldridge replied. "Faerie law is enforced by magic. I cannot say anything because my tongue won't actually say the words. If I even tried, the only sound that would come out would be a wheeze. You have to do this on your own because you're the only mortal here. You're the only one who can break the rules."

"Eldridge," she groaned. "There has to be something. Tell me something, anything that would get me further into her good graces. I've been doing my best and catering to her every whim, but she still looks at me like some new toy. And no one is going to tell a new plaything anything of importance. Not unless it slips out and then we're merely operating on the hope of good luck."

He tapped his finger against his chin, staring off into the distance as he pondered what he might say. Then Eldridge lifted that finger. "She's not the same person she was when I first froze them."

"How so?"

"The price of resurrection is a soul," he replied. Eldridge started pacing back and forth. "The laws of nature are very clear. You don't get to die and come back. That's basic magic. But because she has, I can only assume that the price has something to do with why she's so different. Maybe that's why she's not bringing the rest of her court back either."

"Like she's leaking," Freya said. "Why else would she need to stay in the Winter Court and take magic from you? She already has the power of the Goblin Queen."

Eldridge snapped his fingers and pointed at her. "Precisely. She's here to take as much power as she can, but no one needs this much. Unless she's planning to use it to create another realm." He paused, then shook his head. "No, she wouldn't know how to do that. I was the only one to discover that spell, and I destroyed it after I read it."

"You know how to create other realms?" she asked, dumbfounded.

What kind of magic had he wielded when he was king?

Eldridge shook his head and waved a hand in the air, dismissing her question. "That doesn't matter. I'll tell you some-day. What we need to focus on right now is exposing her weakness. She's hiding something from us, Freya. Something very important to her. Otherwise, she wouldn't be keeping the rest of the court asleep."

Freya tried to remember everything the Queen had told her about her past life. But the Queen was smart. She had revealed nothing personal. Even when they were watching the nightly performance from her dancers, the Queen stayed silent about herself.

Finally, she shrugged in defeat. "I don't know, Eldridge. I don't know what secret she's keeping. Everything is so superficial when we talk."

"Like she suspects that you're trying to uncover something." Eldridge's eyes narrowed.

Arrow snuffled in frustration and sat up. "I think you need to show her you're really working for her. Gain her trust in some big way."

"Like what?" Freya lifted her hands in the air, waving them wildly. "What am I supposed to do now, Arrow? Try to kill the Goblin King in front of her? None of that is going to work because she's still going to see me as a nothing. A no one. A non threat."

They all flinched as a fourth voice interrupted them, echoing like the sound of crushed glass. "That's because you're never going to convince her that you want to help. She's vowed to never trust anyone again. And a faerie vow is binding."

All three of them froze. Freya's eyes widened as she looked over at the tiny ice creature who worked for the Queen. "Frost," she said. "How long have you been there?"

It moved through the wall and stood before them, wringing its hands. "Long enough to know you're searching for a way to beat the Queen."

"Ah." She looked over at Eldridge and knew they both had the same thought.

They needed to destroy the ice creature. As much as it

pained her to admit, Frost was now a liability. He would run to the Queen and tell her everything. And then they would fail.

She stood up from the bed, but Frost held up its hands.

"I want to stop her too," it whispered. "I know you don't trust me, but just listen? Please?"

Freya looked back to Eldridge, who gave a slight nod. Then she looked at Arrow, who sighed and hopped off the bed.

He nudged Frost toward the back of the room where the largest snowdrift was. "You better make yourself a seat then, friend," he said. "We're going to need the entire story from you."

CHAPTER 14

Frost sat on a snow chair he had made himself, with his hands wrapped around an ice mug that looked very much like something a potter would have made. His legs were too short for the chair, so they hung dangling off the edge like a child.

Freya was finding it hard not to think the little creature was adorable. She wanted to wrap her arms around the poor thing and tell it everything would be okay, but that was foolish. This creature worked for the Queen.

Even if he wanted to overthrow her.

She sat on the bed with Arrow to her left, and the Goblin King to her right. They all leaned forward and stared at the ice creature the Queen had made.

She still couldn't fathom how this monster had gotten out of the Queen's magical clutches. It seemed to think for itself, which the other servants most certainly did not do. Maybe it was the power of speech? Perhaps that was what had given Frost the ability to think for itself.

"Well," she started. "Why don't you tell us everything from the beginning."

Frost nodded, staring down into his empty mug before taking

a deep breath. "The Queen didn't make us as servants, at least not a long time ago. We were supposed to be her friends when she was a little girl. She liked to give life to ice and snow because it made her feel more at home."

Eldridge's knee bounced up and down. "I remember that now. She used to name you all and line you up like little soldiers in front of her bedroom. I always had to ask one of you if the Queen would see me if I wanted to play with her."

A soft smile appeared beneath the ice of Frost's face. "I remember that as well. She was much nicer when she was young. Easier to get along with, at the very least." He cleared his throat and then stared back down into the mug. "Then everything changed when she didn't get to become the Goblin Queen. She hated you for taking that from her."

"Of course," Eldridge replied. "She was always power hungry, even back then. She thought she deserved it more than me."

Thoughts bubbled into her memory. Things the Goblin Queen had said that Freya had dismissed, but now she realized were words of insecurity. Or, in their situation, words of weakness.

She leaned forward and braced her forearms on her knees. "She doesn't think she was given the throne the right way now. It's a hard life to believe you have earned respect, but having no one confirm your thoughts about yourself. It must be driving her mad."

"Indeed." Frost nodded along with what she said. "You see, the Queen spent a long time while you were King plotting against you. She wanted to see you ripped from the throne and on your knees before her. That's when everything started getting... dark."

She didn't want to know how dark. Freya had already seen the dancers with bloody feet and the horrible things the Queen could do. Crushed, bloody ice shards would remain in her memory for the rest of her life.

Lifting a hand, she requested, "Can we move past her transgressions? We all know how evil this Queen is. What I want to know is if you have already found out how to beat her. And if you're willing to share that information with us."

Frost nodded vigorously. He kicked his legs up and down. "Yes! There's only one way for the Goblin King or Queen to lose their throne. You can't just take them off of it, because it doesn't work that way."

She didn't follow. They could be taken off their thrones, otherwise Eldridge would still be sitting in the throne room and they wouldn't have to deal with this Queen at all.

Glancing over at Eldridge, she hoped to find a similar expression of confusion on his face. But it wasn't there at all. Instead, he looked very thoughtful as he pondered the ice creature's words.

"You're right," he said. "The throne can only be abdicated by faerie deal or death. Unfortunately, she is unlikely to make any deals that would unseat her. Not like myself."

Freya touched a hand to his bicep. "You still haven't explained why you did that. You bet your entire world on the hope that I wouldn't beat you and then helped me to do so."

The grin on his face made her want to slap him. "You were so interesting, I couldn't help myself. Besides, I could feel her soul rumbling in the ice. I would not be able to keep any of them trapped for very long. This was inevitable."

"So you wanted this to happen?"

Arrow sank his teeth into her forearm and gave her a gentle shake. "We can have this argument later, children. Focus on the ice cube."

Focus on the ice cube? She couldn't focus on anything other than Eldridge having known this would happen, and he still did it. He still chose to lose his throne, his safety, his sanity for what? To draw the Goblin Queen out and hope that Freya could fix his mess for him?

She opened her mouth again to argue, only for Arrow to sink his teeth even deeper in her arm. "Freya," he said, the words garbled through his grip. "Focus on what we can address now. Be mad later."

Letting out a growl that should have made Arrow proud, she wrenched her gaze from the Goblin King and focused on Frost once again. "Do you think she'll make a deal with me?"

The ice monster shook his head. "No. Your king is correct, she's very unlikely to make the same mistake he did. Mortals are too unpredictable and a deal is something she cannot control."

Freya looked between all the faeries and fae-made creatures in the room. Each one wore a matching expression of sadness, and perhaps even expressions of resignation. Why were they all looking like that? If the Queen didn't want to make a deal, then they were back in the same spot they had been.

Weren't they?

She looked over at Arrow and frowned. "Then we've learned nothing new, right? We're stuck?"

"No," he muttered. "There's another option to remove a Goblin King or Queen, but you aren't going to like it."

"Why am I not going to like it?" she asked. Her stomach heaved and what little she'd eaten that day rose once again. Freya already knew the answer. She just didn't want to hear it.

Frost was the one to answer with his grating, horrible voice. "Kill the Queen."

A cold breeze rushed over her entire body. Goosebumps rose on her arms and scattered down her entire body. Freya knew she'd heard him correctly, but his mere idea made her want to vomit.

Kill the Queen? She wasn't a murderer. She didn't know the first thing about ending someone else's life, nor was she interested in learning more. All she wanted was to get out of the Queen's castle and probably take the throne back for Eldridge. Not kill someone.

She lifted her hands up, palms facing the ice monster. "No. I'm not going to kill anyone. There has to be another way."

"There's no other way to take back the throne," Eldridge muttered.

"We can convince her to give it back to you!" Freya shouted and jumped up from her seat, wildly spinning her arms for balance. "She's not a lost cause! The Goblin Queen might be cruel, but you said yourself that she wasn't always like this. We could at the very least try to convince her to do the right thing."

"I don't have that much time, Freya." Eldridge stared up at her with wide eyes. "I know you don't want to hurt anyone. This is difficult for you, and I don't blame you for that. But we have to make a move on the Goblin Queen, and if taking her life is the only way to wrench my crown from her grips..."

Her jaw dropped. Freya asked with a thick voice, "Is this all about the crown for you then?"

Both Arrow and Frost had wide eyes, staring between the two of them as though their parents were arguing. Eldridge opened his mouth, closed it again, then sputtered, "Obviously not."

"Tell me the truth, Eldridge. You set all this up, so that you had to be saved. You knew I was the only person who could actually save you. So is this all about removing the one person who could have fought you for the throne?" She pointed at him and narrowed her gaze into a frown. "Was this all for your pride and greed?"

His mouth gaped open, closed, and then he simply kept his mouth shut.

She felt her stomach drop to her feet. Of course, this wasn't a mistake. He hadn't suddenly become trapped and needed her to save him. He was just using her again, even though the cost was his own pain.

But what king wouldn't be willing to undergo a little pain as long as he got a throne in the end?

Shaking her head, she felt all the tension drain from her shoulders. "At least now I know the truth," she whispered.

"Freya." He stood, reaching out a hand for her to take.

"I'm going to save you still, Goblin King. Don't worry, I will not let you rot because you deceived me. Yet again." She pressed her fingers to her pounding forehead and sighed. "But after this, I am done with you. You can get yourself out of whatever other problems you dig yourself into. I won't save you again. Not after this."

"Freya," he repeated.

She took a hefty step back from him and shook her head. "No, Goblin King. Go back to wherever you came from while we figure out how to kill a Queen."

"You will need my help," he replied angrily.

"No. We won't. What help can you provide when you're locked up in a prison?" She shook her head one last time, then turned her back on him to stare down at Frost.

She knew when he disappeared because the throb in her skull left with him. Then it was just her, Arrow, and Frost left.

Guilt gnawed in her belly. She should have at least been kinder to him. He was, after all, in a prison cell waiting for someone to save him. He could have used the kindness, especially since she had just been preaching that they should give the Goblin Queen a chance to change.

But she couldn't do it. Not after everything they had gone through together, and how easily she knew he manipulated the truth.

Arrow hopped off the bed and sat down at her side, staring up at her while wringing his paws. "I don't know if that was smart, Freya. We still might need his help."

"He's been busting his way into my mind this whole time, Arrow. He's caused me pain, forced me to feel so guilty that I would leave my sister again just to help him. And all of that was because he didn't want to see someone challenge him for the throne. Someone he might not be able to beat." She bit her lip, hoping the stinging pain would prevent her from crying.

And she wanted to cry. Very badly. Freya hadn't done so this entire ordeal since she left her small cottage on the edge of the forest, but she'd never wanted to return to her home more than this moment.

She missed the smell of loam and earth. She missed going to the village and getting her food, rather than hoping a faerie would remember she needed to eat. But mostly she missed being around other humans and knowing what to expect when she was talking to them.

Freya needed to pull herself together. There was more to be done and she couldn't fall apart yet.

But she was very ready to have her moment where she could finally let the tears flow. She would greatly love that moment for the release of all this pain and anguish in her chest.

She took a deep, steadying breath, then sat back down onto the bed.

"Frost," she said. "How do we kill the Queen?"

CHAPTER 15

Freya followed Frost through the castle in the middle of the night. She'd never left her room at this wee hour in the morning. And now she was happy that she never had.

All the lights in the castle dimmed as the Queen slept. Some disappeared entirely until they were walking through the halls, relying on radiant light from other areas of the castle.

The darkness made the ice more terrifying. Sometimes she could hear a deep groan echoing through the walls. Her mind spun nightmares of some ancient creature trapped underneath the castle, and its pain traveled through the ice.

At least they were moving quietly. She'd put on her old clothing, the brown coloring made her easier to overlook. Besides, these clothes were much warmer than what the Goblin Queen had provided her. And the boots were more comfortable than soft, rabbit lined slippers.

"Are you sure we're going the right way?" she whispered.

"Yes," Frost replied. They had covered his feet with some of Freya's old clothing so the ice wouldn't tap as they walked. "It's just this way."

A small part of her worried that the ice creature was bringing her back to the Queen. He was, after all, made by the Goblin Queen's magic. Surely it would be impossible for him to go against her wishes.

Frost had explained that magic always had a price. Sometimes, like giving him a voice, it meant that her control would break. He was a free thinking creation now, and he didn't like what the Queen was doing.

The explanation seemed a bit of a stretch to her. But she didn't know all that much about magic and knew better than to question those who did.

They stopped in front of an icy door and he pointed at it. "This is the door. Go straight through the snow and you'll find a bog. Don't talk to any of the faeries within it. Touch nothing other than the compass at the center. That will bring you to the weapon you seek."

Weapon. It still sent shivers down her spine. Was she entertaining killing someone because she couldn't imprison them?

Killing the Queen wouldn't be easy. The Goblin Queen knew how to say the right words that wiggled into Freya's mind. All she could hope was that in the moment when she needed to take action, that she would. Freya feared she would freeze.

With a sharp nod, she pulled the hood of her cloak up and over her head, then buttoned it tight around her neck. "How cold is it going to be out there?"

Frost gave her an unimpressed stare. "Freezing."

Of course, it would be. Why had she even asked the question?

Freya yanked the door open and plunged out into the waist deep snow. The mountain loomed over her head, dark and ominous now that she knew what it hid within it. But the sheer cliff of the mountain stopped here, and the ground was a great tundra of snow and nothing else. A blizzard raged over her head, but none of the snow touched her. Almost as though the blizzard wasn't actually there at all.

Frowning, she tugged her hood down and tried to step in a

straight line. She often had to turn around and stare behind her, double checking that her footprints were orderly. It was hard to tell, but she assumed they were.

The blizzard made everything white. The sky, the ground, everything her eyes could see. Eventually, even the mountain disappeared from view.

"Keep going straight," she whispered to herself. The raging blizzard overhead stole her words and tossed them over her shoulder. The wind was bitter and ruthless, never giving her a second to breathe. Or at least, that's what it felt like.

Freya had no idea how long she struggled through the blizzard and the ice. It could have been mere moments, hours, or even days. But when the wind stopped howling, she knew she had reached her destination.

Another mountain, though much smaller, appeared in the distance. The monolithic structure was surrounded by what looked like hot springs. Tiny dots in the distance broke through the snow and the ice at her feet. The blizzard didn't touch that place, it seemed. Snow still blasted all around her, whipping her hair in all directions, but it stopped in a wall of white. Raging in one area, but if she stepped through the storm, it would be silent on the other side.

The moment she stepped out of the blizzard, all the raging sounds of the storm stopped. Disappearing as though it had never existed at all. The howling winds dropped away and then... nothing.

The silence was terrifying.

Swallowing hard, she trudged through the snow until she reached the very edge of the hot springs. She knew this was the place Frost had spoken of, yet it still felt as though she were intruding upon something that no mortal was supposed to see.

Frost had claimed this was a swamp. The hot springs were more like pits with bubbling water that had a thin layer of goo on the top. Each bubble took a while to build, then even longer to pop. A fine layer of algae grew on the top, but the green coloring was too minty for it to be familiar. Pale and thin, the thick scum on the water shouldn't have grown there at all.

She stepped over a few stones, picking her way through the bog. Her feet sank into the thick mossy ground. She lifted her foot and felt the ground suctioning her boot.

"Careful, Freya," she reminded herself. "If you fall into this water, you'll freeze solid."

Moving through the bog was a little easier than she'd expected, although she had to backtrack many times. The paths through the hot springs sometimes ended. Pools would collide with each other, and she'd have to choose another way.

Freya didn't know what she was looking for. A compass, is what Frost said, but he hadn't given her any idea how to find the darn thing. He'd made it seem like it would be obvious where it was. Obviously, he did not know how difficult it would end up being to find.

A cough echoed over the bubbling water. Freya froze where she was, one leg lifted to take a step. Her brown skirts swayed around her and slowly, she turned to look to her left.

Three faeries were huddled inside one of the pools. Their skin was covered in a fine layer of pale green mud, cracking where they hadn't dunked their bodies underneath the warm water in a while. The one in the middle had her arms around the other two who looked like they were male.

Their ears were incredibly long, almost longer than their entire head. They wore no clothing at all, just the layer of mud.

She wanted to take her cloak off and give it to one of them. Or all three.

Freya opened her mouth to tell them to get out of the water. That was step one. If they could get dry, then they could find something to put on and then huddle near the warm water, but not within it.

Then she remembered Frost had told her not to talk to anyone. She couldn't speak with any of the faeries in this place, although he hadn't given her a reason why.

Perhaps they were dangerous. Or maybe this was a curse that would pass on to her if she tried to converse with any of them. Freya didn't know, but she knew the faerie realm was a very dangerous place. What looked like it was impossible was very possible, as the Goblin King would say.

The thought of him made her shiver and step around the pool with the three faeries in it. Even though she was still angry at him for setting this all in motion, she also realized why he'd done it. This was the only way to bring the Goblin Queen out of her hiding. He had few choices, didn't he?

Stomping through the muck, she came upon two more pools with faeries. One held a single occupant who shivered uncontrollably, holding his arms around his head. A faint whining sound could be heard, although she wasn't sure if he was trying to speak or if he was crying. The third pool was full of faeries. Ten, eleven, she couldn't count because they were all massed together.

Who were these creatures?

Freya noticed there was a small podium in the distance, but she couldn't figure out how to get there. That had to be where the compass was held. It was surrounded by many pools filled with the mud covered faeries with only a single path to get to it.

Goal in mind, she squared her shoulders and figured out the maze to get to where she needed to go.

It took a little while to retrace her steps. She paused a few times with her finger in her air, tracing the lines of the path that she could see. But finally, she made it to the path that would take her to the podium.

A small compass rested on top of the stone structure. She was so happy to see that it wasn't made out of ice, she planned to kiss the stone when she reached it.

Lifting a foot, she went to set it down, only to freeze at the last second when one of the faeries lunged forward. It slapped a muddy hand onto the moss before her and glared at Freya with hatred in its eyes.

"None may pass," it rasped.

She had to pass. This faerie wasn't going to stop her.

If she wasn't supposed to talk to them, then she wouldn't entertain this threat. However, Freya assumed she also wasn't supposed to touch them. Why couldn't this have been a little easier?

There wasn't another way over the path. She reached into her pockets and tried to find something she could give the faerie that might convince it. There were just a few bits of bread and dried fruit that she'd grabbed to keep her stomach full on the journey. Nothing else was useful.

She pulled out a handful of raisins and let them drop from her fingers into the outstretched hand.

The faerie blinked its enormous eyes and twitched its ears. It looked down at the raisins, then retreated into the waters. The dried fruit was held in its hands like she'd given the faerie gold coins.

Maybe that was the secret. These creatures obviously hadn't eaten in a very long time. They were all emaciated and shivering in the water. Surely that would be her way to get them to leave her alone?

She took one step onto the moss and then stopped again when another faerie's hand darted in front of her. Over and over, she handed them bits of food, making sure not to touch them or utter a single sound.

The food ran out before the faeries. There were still three more, each watching her with hungry eyes. Her heart broke for them.

Don't apologize, she told herself. Say nothing until you're in front of that damn podium.

Freya gathered her skirts in her hands, took a running start, and leapt over the faerie's outstretched hands. They shrieked in anger, but at the very least she had gotten to the podium.

The ground was more sturdy here. As though the moss had grown over stone instead of dirt. She stomped her foot to make sure it wasn't ice, and that she wasn't about to fall into a trap, but nothing happened.

The compass sat on top of the podium, unsuspecting with no guards or visible wards. It looked like a normal metal compass. The same kind she'd seen a hundred times in her life.

Hesitantly, she reached out, then snatched it off the podium. She waited for something to happen. Some big, booming sound that would echo all around her. Or perhaps the hot springs would overflow and she'd have to run from the boiling water and the faeries who were released.

But nothing happened at all.

She stared down at the compass and the pin that swirled in her hand. It wasn't pointing north, that was for certain. Instead, it seemed to be wildly moving and waiting for something.

Magic. She'd never get used to it.

Leaning close to the metal, she whispered, "I need to find the weapon that will kill the Goblin Queen."

The pin stopped spinning. It pointed behind the podium at a wall of pale green ivy that had seen better days. Narrowing her eyes suspiciously, she stepped closer to the ivy. It moved with a wind that she didn't feel, so she could only assume...

Freya reached out and brushed some of the tangled plants aside. Thorns bit into the mittens on her hands, sticking to the wool. She didn't care. Because there was a cave hidden behind the plants. A cold, damp cave that was full of darkness.

She frowned into the shadows. No one would walk into that without some kind of light or a torch. She needed something.

But when she looked around, she realized there was nothing to give her light. No sticks. No fire. Nothing.

And this was the only chance they had at stopping this horrible Queen and saving the Goblin King. So even though she was terrified, Freya plunged into the darkness. She only hoped there wasn't something waiting for her.

CHAPTER 16

Once her eyes adjusted to the darkness, she could see vague shadows and shapes around herself, although she had no idea what they were. They could be stones. They could have been armored fae watching her every move.

The compass had a small light within it. The needle glowed on its own and never wavered from the same direction it always seemed to point. So she used that as a guide to get through the tunnels of the cave until she burst out into an enormous cavern.

Sunlight speared from a slight crack at the top of the cave and illuminated the stones. Small mossy patches shone emerald green and were brighter than the sun itself. Or perhaps she was so starved for color, that anything looked vibrant.

Golden sun slashes caught on a stone giant embedded into the rock walls. Only his outstretched hand and bowed head poked through the mountain. The rest was hidden within the stone. Bald, with a polished skull, he stared down at the ground as though defeated in battle long ago.

She wondered what the giant's story was. If the carving was created by an artist, then the emotion was so painful and pure it made her heart ache. But she had a feeling a person hadn't created this masterpiece. This was the faerie realm, after all, and this giant was most likely an actual person who had once been alive.

Freya thought it possible that the Goblin Queen had turned this man into stone. Maybe it was the Goblin Queen's parents, although a giant such as this would have been depicted in the tapestries.

He didn't look like the kind of person who attacked villages or castles. The soft expression of sadness on his face was one she had only seen in the kindest of souls. He held out his hand as though waiting for something. Or someone.

She stepped down into the cave, remaining as quiet as possible because she wasn't sure if she was supposed to talk yet. Could she speak to this creature? Or was that breaking the rules yet again?

She reached out and held onto his thumb that was as tall as Freya. Hauling herself up onto his palm, she walked forward and saw there was a small inscription in the center of his hand. Someone had carved into his stone flesh, "Warm the giant, and he shall provide all you seek."

At least she knew she could talk to him.

Freya looked around for something that might heat this great being. There was a compact bundle of sticks where someone had once built a fire, not in the hand, but at least close enough. She hopped down and gathered it all up in her arms.

A flint laid nestled between stones, with a small leather thong attached to it. She tried very hard not to think about the people who had come here before her.

She stepped back up onto the hand and set her wood into a pattern that she knew would catch ablaze. Putting her hands on her hips, she surveyed her work and then nodded. "That will do."

Carefully stepping back down onto the floor, she returned to the flint and leaned down to pick it up. She lifted it, and a rattling sound startled her. Freya stared in horror at the skeletal hand still clutching the flint in its grasp.

With a shriek, she dropped the flint and shook her hands to

rid herself of the shock. She hadn't noticed the bones poking out of the ground where the flint had laid, but apparently someone else had already tried this way to wake up the giant.

They had failed. But she still had to try.

Shaking the skeletal fingers off the flint, she settled her nerves once more. "Stop it, Freya. At least you'll get warm even if this won't wake the giant."

She'd think about this later. And she knew in that moment, she would grow ill knowing she had touched a dead body. Perhaps she would even vomit. But for now, she would start a fire and hope this time, a fire was all the giant wanted.

Using the giant's hand as a lever, she heaved herself back up onto the great palm and set to work building a large campfire. Once the roaring flames crackled, she sat down near the warmth and tried to get some feeling back in her numb fingers.

It was hard to get comfortable in this place. She couldn't even heat her own body up, let alone a giant like this. How was she supposed to thaw the ice that had dripped from his nose and frosted his brows?

She'd need a fire big enough to fill the entire cavern. And then she'd choke herself with smoke after the attempt. It would take her months to gather that much wood, anyway.

"There has to be another way to warm you," she muttered. "Now, what is it?"

Warming a person might not be physical. Freya was always warm in her very soul when she talked about the things she loved. Maybe that was what the giant was waiting for. He wanted a story that would warm him from the inside out.

It was worth a try. And a better plan than she'd come up with thus far.

Freya wrapped her arms around her legs and hugged them close to her chest. What story did she tell first? There were a lot of stories that made her heart squeeze in her chest, but none of them would interest a giant. She wasn't someone who had created a life story worth listening to.

"When I was little, my mother used to take me into the forest," she started. "She didn't like being in the shadows of the trees, but she always brought me there to teach me how to live on my own. Just in case I ever found myself lost in the woods.

"One day, when I had wandered too far from my mother's side, I heard her calling for me in the bushes. I knew nothing about faeries at that point. So I wandered away without worrying what might wait for me. I didn't notice the slight differences in the words, and how the voice didn't sound exactly like my mother.

"I remember her crashing through the brush, screaming my name. And instead of getting mad when she found me, likely just before some faerie had kidnapped me, she pulled me into her arms. I will never forget the love in her voice when she told me I was the most important thing in her life. And that losing me would feel like losing her own heart."

Instead, her mother had forced her children to lose her instead.

Freya frowned. That memory had always heated her to the very soul, and yet, it wasn't doing that at all. She was sad when she remembered it now. She feared what had happened to her mother, and all she could think about was living with her sister on their own. Her mother had spent so many years worrying about losing her children, only to make them suffer the very fate she had tried to avoid.

No, that memory wouldn't do. The giant would only pity her for a childhood ill spent.

Clearing her throat, she tried a different memory. One that always made her laugh.

"My sister lived with me my entire life. She's always been my shadow, right there with me, even when I didn't want her to be. When she was just a child, she used to put frogs in my pockets because she liked to hear me scream."

Freya grinned, this time remembering how much she loved being with her little sister. "She'd fill my drawers with snakes every chance she had. Sometimes, in the middle of the night, I'd catch her in the window talking to the spiders outside. She's always been more interested in things that made other people uncomfortable. Or even afraid."

Like goblins who kidnapped little girls and stole them away to a faerie realm. A magical place full of dangers and monsters. Or, if the little girls were lucky, full of Goblin Kings and fairytale quests.

Yet again, she discovered this place had tainted another memory. She couldn't feel warm about the thought of her sister in the mortal realm when she knew just how much Esther had hated living in that place. Now that Esther wanted to remain here, thinking of her in their home felt... wrong.

She imagined her sister back home, where Esther had felt like she wasn't free, and her stomach turned. Freya couldn't bear to put Esther in a cage again. Not after everything her sister had accomplished.

Frustrated, she tucked a strand of hair behind her ear and tried to think of another story. Anything that was from her old life that might have made her feel better, and thus inspired the giant to come alive.

She couldn't think of a single thing.

The strand of hair fell back in front of her face, pulled out of place by a warm hand.

"I was wondering when you would show back up," she muttered, putting the hair back behind her ear so it wouldn't distract her any more.

"I always show up when you need me," the Goblin King said. His breath played along the back of her neck, hot and warm and all too distracting. "After all, you're out here telling a giant stories of the mortal realm. You already know what stories you should tell him to heat his soul."

"I don't know what you're talking about." But the words were a lie. She knew what the Goblin King wanted her to say. There were only a few memories that left her breathless, and he knew all of them.

After all, he'd been there for each one of them.

His claws dragged over the fabric of her cloak and down her shoulders. "Why don't you try telling him about me, Freya?"

"He's not interested in learning about the Goblin King. I don't think a giant would care very much about your story."

"He doesn't care about me. Or my story. What he cares about is feeling some warmth in that icy soul of yours." He leaned closer and whispered his next words in her ear. "Or have you been in the Winter Court so long that you've forgotten what passion feels like?"

"Stop it," she breathed. "Thoughts of you don't make me feel passion."

"We both know that's a lie."

The Goblin King disappeared back to whatever prison he was in, but his presence still lingered. The scent of him. The feeling of his fingers on her body.

Rolling her eyes, she let the story of the Goblin King tumble from between her lips. She told the giant everything, holding nothing back. How she was confused by the attention of an immortal faerie, but also how it made her heart sing that he would give her any attention at all.

She was nothing and no one. He saw something in her that had captured his attention, and she really didn't understand why.

But his kisses were amazing.

And she hadn't stopped thinking about his lips since he had kissed her. That was problematic. She hadn't ever entertained a man before and adding that stress to this quest only made every-thing that much more difficult. She didn't want to think about a man when she had a job to do. Freya was better at focusing on what had to be done, rather than what could be done.

The fingers surrounding her twitched, shifted, then curled in toward her. Gently, the giant lifted his arm from the rocks and raised her closer to his face. "You're only feeling conflicted about this because you've never felt this way before. It's perfectly natural to be confused when you have no idea what is happening. You need to give yourself a break."

She stared up into the eyes that were larger than her torso and gulped. A giant was talking to her. A very kind, albeit extremely large, giant who was frozen in the side of a mountain just a few moments ago.

Yet, her story was the one that had woken this fantastical creature. And it wasn't her warmed soul or passion for the Goblin King that had convinced the giant to wake up.

It was that she needed someone to talk to about her relationship with the Goblin King. She needed advice.

Apparently, that advice would come from the lips of a giant.

CHAPTER 17

Freya stared up into the eyes of the giant and tried to close her jaw. Goodness, he was big. Bigger than a house and even larger than some of the castles she had seen in this faerie realm. He held her so carefully, like he knew how easily he could crush her, but didn't want to scare her.

She appreciated that.

Clearing her throat, she stuck out her hand as though he might shake it. "Freya of Woolwich."

"Nice to meet you, Freya. Now why don't you tell me more about this Goblin King that you're falling in love with?" He grinned, revealing chipped teeth that looked as stoney as the rest of his visage.

She frowned. "I'm not falling in love with the Goblin King."

"You most certainly are. I'm afraid that's just how it goes when you're around someone as much as you two have been. It sounds like there's a rather extensive amount of sparks, as well. Have you thought about talking to him about your feelings?" The ground rumbled, and he pulled his other hand out of the earth.

The giant cavern it revealed beneath him made her head spin. If she took one step in the wrong direction, then she would tumble into that dark hole. What would happen then? Would she plunge to her death, breaking every bone in her body before she settled in a mess of broken bones and scrambled flesh?

He must have noticed her staring. The giant shifted her away from the hole, then propped his head on the other hand. Leaning against his fist, he tilted his head to the side and then shook his hand.

She stumbled, apparently moving as he wanted.

The giant asked, "Well? Are you going to admit it or not?"

"Admit what?" she reached out and held onto his thumb for balance. "That I'm falling in love with the Goblin King? I'm not."

"Then why did it disappoint you so much to hear he'd put himself in danger? If you didn't care for him, you would have recognized it as the smartest decision he could make to flush out the Goblin Queen. You would have seen the logic in his choice." The giant lifted a brow.

She disagreed. But a sickly feeling made her stomach turn, because what if he was right? "Are you suggesting if I were falling in love with him, that he isn't feeling the same? And that's why he could put me in danger to save his throne?"

The giant rolled its eyes. "My dear, is there any reason for you to think he doesn't view you as in high regard? He has moved space and time for you. He trusts you to be the only person who could save him from the Goblin Queen. So much so that he actually went through with this insane plan."

Right. And she had just as good as admitted the giant was correct and that she was falling wildly in love with this Goblin King.

Sighing, she flopped down into his palm and cradled her head in her hands. "What am I going to do? I can't be considering this. He's a faerie. I'm a human. We don't mix."

"Historically you mix very well." The giant's cheek squished as his palm shoved it up. "You see, most goblins marry mortal women. Their animal bloodline gets a little too strong if they don't, and faerie blood always overrides mortal blood. It's as easy as that."

She dropped her hands from her face and stared up at the giant again. "How much do you know about goblins? Or the courts?"

"Everything." The giant looked pointedly around them. "This is the Chamber of Memories, my dear. I watch everything that happens in the realm. Nothing is said, done, or thought about without me knowing of it. That's why you're here. I'm the only living person who knows where the knife was hidden."

Freya waved her hand in the air, dismissing the knife entirely. They'd get to that. But first, she wanted to find out everything she could about the Goblin King and the very new Queen.

"The Queen said Eldridge used to live with them in the castle. But there's something that I just don't understand. Her hatred for him runs deep. So deep I have a hard time believing it's because he took the goblin throne from her."

"You haven't pieced that together yet?" he asked. His eyes squeezed shut and his lips turned down at the corners. "Eldridge always saw her as his adopted sister. And though they were of similar age, he considered himself to be part of the Winter Court when they took him. It was as simple as that in his mind, and he never considered another future."

Though the thought had occurred to her, Freya hadn't given it any merit until this moment. "But the Goblin Queen... She didn't view him as a sibling, did she?"

The giant shook his head. "No. In her mind, he was always the Autumn Thief. A very handsome, very strange young man who had appeared from another court. And he catered to her every whim, as he thought a good brother should do. They went riding together. He taught her how to prank her parents, and he marveled at the ice magic she could control when she was but a child. They were inseparable."

She shouldn't feel pity for the Goblin Queen, but she did. A strange mixture of emotions pulsed in her chest.

Jealousy because she didn't want anyone else to have claim to the Goblin King. She didn't enjoy hearing about another woman who had been such an important part of his life. But she also realized just how tempting he could be. How the thought of his arms around her had consumed her mind so easily.

The Goblin Queen had only hoped for something more from the young man who had come into her court. Instead, she had been given a brother who would remain a brother no matter how hard she tried to convince him that she wasn't his blood relative.

Such unrequited love could destroy a person. Or, in the Goblin Queen's case, make them hell bent for revenge.

Freya sighed, all her emotions filtering out with the breath. "So she loved him, then."

"In whatever way the Goblin Queen could love anyone. Her heart is cruel, Freya. I wish I could say she was once a good person, but she always leaned toward darkness and pain." The giant moved his hand, wiggling his fingers until she stepped off of him and back onto the ground. "You should not feel guilty for what you are about to do. The last remaining good part of her wants this as well."

"I find that hard to believe." She stared around them at the cave and the moss that dripped from the rocks. This place couldn't really be so cruel as to let a woman die because she'd loved the wrong person? "I don't think she wants to die. I think she wants revenge."

"And then what?" The giant waved his hand in the air. "She won't stop there. Revenge is an empty plan. Once she gets it, then where will she go? What will she focus on? The next person who harmed her? You need to see what she was like during the faerie wars. Perhaps then you will understand why I say she needs to rest. Forever."

Freya remembered what Eldridge had written in his journal. The faerie wars were brutal, yes, but the nobility of the Winter Court had remained in their castle. He had done what he could to protect them on the battlefield. But none of them were out there with him.

She opened her mouth to argue, but the giant interrupted her with an all knowing stare.

"Freya," he muttered. "Do you believe everything you found in a journal? Of course the Goblin Queen fought. This was her court and people were trying to take her from the throne. They wanted to murder her and her family. The fight was exactly what she wanted. She fought with her soldiers, side by side, and she never stopped fighting. She loved the bloodshed."

"I..." What was she supposed to do with this knowledge?

Freya didn't know why it was even important for her to believe the Goblin Queen was a bad person. After all, there was no other way out of this. Eldridge, Arrow, Frost, they all had said the Queen had to die.

And Freya was the only one who could kill her, apparently, even though she had never killed anyone in her life.

Frustrated, she wrapped her arms around herself and muttered, "I don't know why it's so important for me to believe this. Does it matter if I think she's an evil person or not?"

"It does," the giant replied. "Because you cannot hesitate. And if you don't truly believe that this is the only way, you will. She has lived hundreds of years. All that time gave her experience that you could never dream of. If you want to beat her, Freya, then you must not question your resolve."

Freya was already questioning it. She questioned everything the fae told her because none of it sounded like the truth. Even though she knew some of it had to be. Or at least the vague shadow of truth when they were always trying to hide something.

Hesitation was part of how she had survived this world.

"Freya," the giant groaned. "Perhaps it would be best if you simply saw what she has done. I fear everything rests on your shoulders now, and that you don't realize just how important this is."

"Of course I do." Freya wanted to argue that she had listened. Everyone kept telling her what to do and how to do it, but she was certain this wasn't right. There was more she could do. More that they could at least attempt to convince the Goblin Queen to listen.

Why were they all giving up on this woman who had wanted to be loved?

But she didn't get the chance to argue. The giant shifted and pulled himself out of the mountain. The ground grumbled in anger, shaking beneath her feet and rocking her dangerously close to the edge of the abyss from which the giant emerged.

He lifted a hand and slammed it down on the other edge of the cave. The wall shifted, then broke as if someone had punched a hole through the stone itself. Light speared through the space, revealing an enormous field on the other side filled with fog and drifting clouds.

A field that was barren of snow, though still dusted with pale greys and whites.

"What is this place?" she asked.

"It is the final battleground of the faerie wars," the giant said. "Many faeries died here. And sometimes when a faerie dies in a gruesome manner, they don't leave the spot where they met their demise. No matter how many people try to convince them to leave, they will remain exactly where they died. You need to speak with these remnants of a time long past."

She didn't want to talk to ghosts. Freya had already talked with faeries, and that was more than enough for her lifetime.

"Spirits?" She said the word as though it were a curse.

"In a manner of speaking. They are quiet souls who have no desire to harm you, Freya. They merely want to talk." The giant pointed toward the opening in the cave. "Go. There is no other way out."

She didn't want to. But apparently, like everything she'd experienced in the faerie realms since coming here, Freya didn't have a choice. She had to go through this hole in the wall. Speak with the ghosts like that was something she did every day.

"I don't know why I need to be convinced," she grumbled. "I just need the knife."

"And they are the only ones who will tell you where it is, now. I certainly won't." The giant quirked a brow. "They will bring you to it if they deem you worthy."

"Another test." Freya picked her way over the stones and out onto the fog covered fields. "It's always another test in this place."

CHAPTER 18

Freya stepped onto the ashen fields and heard the stones knitting themselves back together behind her. She didn't turn to look. There was no need anymore, magic was simply what it was. She didn't worry about it anymore, even though it still felt a little strange to see sometimes.

Compared to the cave, this place was eerily quiet. She hadn't realized just how loud the sound of dripping water and the giant's breath had been.

This place had no sound at all.

No wind.

No breath.

Nothing but the faint hush of ash shifting in a breeze that was sluggish and low. The grey clumps on the ground looked almost like snow. It was so thick a blanket that the ash covered whatever was lying beneath the surface.

Although Freya knew what the ash hid. She wasn't so naïve that she couldn't guess what remained on this battlefield.

She stepped over what looked like a ribcage. Bodies laid everywhere. Some of them were completely bare, leaving just the hint of bones and what might have once been a person. Others didn't have a body left at all, but their armor remained where they had once lain.

Swallowing hard, she bent down and picked up a shoulder plate. The silver had been polished once, but now was dingy with age. Fine filigree decorated the edges, standing out against the flat metal. Tiny dots and swirls might have meant something once to this person who had worn it. A family crest, perhaps.

The person had died wearing this armor that was supposed to protect them. They had given up everything for this war and their court, only to fall here and then be forgotten.

Footsteps behind her proceeded the scent of apple pie. Eldridge stepped to her side, and she realized he didn't leave any footprints in the ash. He bent down as well, sinking onto his haunches, and reached out his hand to touch a small pile of ash.

Peering closer, she could make out the shape of a skull beneath his hand. The teeth still stood out in stark relief, even though the ash looked like a white blanket had been laid over the head.

"This was where it all happened," he said. His voice was full of haunted memories. "The last stand as all the courts battled with each other because we all refused to admit there was only one person worthy of being the Goblin King."

"Why?" she asked. "Why wouldn't they all fall in line under a single person?"

"Because every court wanted someone from their own to take the throne. It was the first year in recorded history that it might be possible. The Autumn Court had always given up their Thief to become the King or Queen. But that year it could have been anyone from any season." He stared down at the skull as though it could look up at him. "And it was partly my fault. I didn't want to take the throne, and I made that very clear. I gave them false hope."

He turned his head, and she gasped in horror. The side of his face that had been turned away from her was horrifically burned. The ragged edges of blistered skin stretched all the way into his hairline. It was the worst around his eye, where someone had clearly tried to take out the orb.

"What happened?" she whispered, reaching out a hand to touch him.

"The same thing that has been happening since she first captured me, Freya. Nothing new." He leaned away from her touch. "Did you not hear me? All this life lost is my fault. I was the one who encouraged them to battle and I am the one to hold the weight of this guilt."

She looked around the battlefield and saw all the carnage that had once been here. "Perhaps you do," she replied. "But do you not dishonor all the souls who were once here by not taking the throne again? You were a good king, Eldridge. Everyone I've spoken with agrees. They love you as their monarch, and they want you back."

"I suppose that's what every king wants, isn't it? To prove we're worthy of their adoration." He stood up slowly, as if the movement pained him. "I didn't want you to see these memories. The giant knew that."

"You don't always get what you want." Freya stood as well. "The giant said I needed to see it for myself. So I don't make some mistake that we're incapable of reversing, I guess."

"Like not killing the Goblin Queen when you have the chance?" There was something in his gaze that she couldn't name. Some emotion that was almost like hope, but poisoned with regret.

"Why are you so sad?" she asked, taking a step forward. Eldridge retreated from her. She took another step closer to him and chased him through the ashen fields. "I don't think I've ever seen you like this. Do you not want her to die?"

Something twisted in her chest. Maybe he had buried all that emotion in his heart for so long and was just now realizing that he was in love with the Goblin Queen. That he had denied her his attention for such a long time, but that he hadn't wanted to deny her at all.

What if this was his revelation and now Freya was just standing in the way?

She could return to the mortal world. Without her sister, of course, because Esther had already started making a life for herself here.

Why did that hurt so much? The mere idea of leaving with no one to come home to stung, but it wasn't that emotion that churned in her belly. It was the jealousy and the heartbreak that maybe she was too late.

The anger that he had put himself in danger and used her as an escape. That emotion had made her too late to tell him how she really felt. She couldn't do anything other than accept whatever his choice was. Because she couldn't control him.

Swallowing hard, Freya stopped where she was. "If you don't want me to kill her, then we can find another way. Perhaps you two can share the throne. Perhaps—"

"No." He stepped forward and caught her around the waist.

Eldridge tucked her into the curve of his body. Those starry eyes swirled, hypnotic and oh so very enthralling. Freya couldn't breathe when he looked at her like that.

"I know you two were close when you were children," she whispered. "The giant told me a lot of things. And I think you need to reconcile that history with her before you make any decisions. Maybe she doesn't have to die."

"You are willing to give up so much to save someone who means nothing to you." He lifted a hand between them and tunneled his hand into her hair. "That heart is part of the reason I am so fascinated with you, Freya. You choose to forgive and to allow people to live their lives even though it may make yours harder."

"It's not always about me," she replied with a shrug. "I can give up some of my comfort as long as it helps someone else in the long run."

"And that is very unfaerie-like of you." He sighed, the breath fanning across her lips. "I know you're mad at me, Freya.

You have every right to be. But if there could have been another way for me to do this, you must know that I would have chosen that path. I would have done anything to spare you this pain."

She didn't know that, not really. Even now, a part of Freya didn't believe that he would have changed anything. He knew how to manipulate and warp the truth into something that suited him. That included changing reality.

But she knew she was already tired of being angry with him. She was so exhausted and the safety his arms provided was so tempting. Even though she knew it was only temporary.

Freya rested her head on his shoulder, taking the comfort he offered. "I know you aren't really here right now, but I wish you were."

She felt the press of his lips against her hair. Those lips curved into a smile that spread heat from the top of her head to the bottom of her toes.

Eldridge chuckled. "Don't tell me you're growing fond of my presence, my hero."

"I wouldn't go so far as to say that." Of course she was. She shouldn't have allowed herself to think like that at all, but... She was.

Every time he was with her, she felt stronger. Like she could do more than the average mortal.

And then she remembered her jealousy when she had thought he might want the Goblin Queen more than her. Even though it was all in her head, she felt like she might have lost him only a few moments ago. And this was her chance.

If she didn't want to lose him, then she had to say something. She had to admit her feelings or it was entirely possible that he would decide it wasn't worth it to chase her through the faerie courts again.

Even if it made her pride sting to be the first one to admit it.

Freya sighed into his shoulder and shook her head. "Actually, I think I might like having you around."

"Excuse me?" He reared back in surprise. "Are you admitting that you're fond of me?"

"I'm admitting that looking at you doesn't make me sick to my stomach." No, that wasn't the right way to say it. She wasn't a child. Freya cleared her throat. "And that, maybe things are better when you're around."

He leaned closer, his eyes locked on her lips. "Is that so? I'll admit, I've been waiting to hear those words for some time now."

"We don't have time for this." She stared at the berry red color of his mouth and wished there was more time.

She wanted to taste him again, to feel his hands on her body and see what a faerie king could do with those long fingers. After all, she wasn't a child anymore. When she might have been afraid of a Goblin King in her younger years, now she wanted to know what he desired.

His lips barely brushed hers in a featherlight touch, like a butterfly resting against her for a mere moment. "If only there was more time. I would convince you that you should never leave this place. But we have company, and I'm afraid ignoring the dead is a poor decision."

The dead?

Her mind was so foggy she couldn't imagine what he was talking about. She wanted him to kiss her again. A real kiss this time, not just some feather touch that left her wanting more.

Then the word pierced through the fog of her mind and she remembered they were standing in the middle of a battlefield. Particularly one that was known to be very, very haunted.

Gasping, she lurched out of his arms and spun around. Eldridge had been staring over her shoulder. She could only imagine what was behind her.

The spectral figure was ethereal and delicate. The silver edges of its form moved in the wind, though she couldn't make out who or what the creature was. It wore a cloak covering its head and face. The spirit rode the ancient ghost of a reindeer that was slowly rotting. Freya tried hard not to stare at the skull of the steed that lacked any flesh.

The cloak draped over the body of the reindeer, and the spirit reached forward to use the beast's horns as reins to direct the beast toward Freya and Eldridge.

The strange rider stopped a mere ten feet from the only two living people on a battlefield of the dead.

"Why have you come?" it asked. The rumbling tones were deep and rode the wind like the howl of a wolf.

"I need to know how to kill the Goblin Queen," she replied. She stepped out of Eldridge's arms and closer to the ghost. "I was sent here to relive her memories so that I could see why she needs to be removed from the throne."

Although, it seemed like everyone feared Freya wouldn't do what needed to be done.

The spirit inclined its head, the hood shifting just enough for her to see the white skull beneath it. "So be it. If you wish to have the weapon, then you must know what happened to us. You must see for yourself the torment."

She swallowed hard and looked to Eldridge for one last reassurance. Except Eldridge wasn't there anymore. He had disappeared, returning to wherever his torture was enacted.

Freya was alone in this, again. Only this time she was certain she would succeed.

Straightening her back and squaring her shoulders, she returned her attention to the ghost before her. "I accept that I need to experience to understand. Please, lead the way and I will follow."

CHAPTER 19

The spirit reached out its hand for her to take. "Come with me, Freya of Woolwich. Hero of the Autumn Court and beloved by the Goblin King."

Beloved? She felt the blood drain from her face.

"Oh, no," she corrected. "He doesn't..."

"Stop talking," the ghost scolded. "You said you wanted to experience it. And experience you shall. But there will be no more arguing or trying to explain your beliefs. I am dead. Trust in the knowledge of the spirit realm and allow us to show you what the real history of this place is."

She clamped her jaw shut and stared at the bones of his hand. There were a few grisly pieces of flesh still hanging from him, and she could only assume that his body was around here somewhere. If she wasn't careful, she might even step on it.

Swallowing all her fear, she nodded and took the boney hand. "Show me everything."

Freya had expected to travel again. She had thought the ghost would bring her to yet another place. Instead, touching him allowed her to see into the spirit realm. Thus she was forced to watch as a thousand faerie souls all burst into view.

They fought with wild abandon. Their swords gleaming in

sunlight she couldn't feel. The sound of axes striking shields was so overwhelming she could hardly even hear her own thoughts.

A great beast, perhaps an orc or troll, swung a hammer over her head. She ducked down low, but the hammer never touched her. Instead, it collided with the skull of a beautiful pixie behind her. She watched in horror as the other warrior's head exploded.

Flinching away, she closed her eyes and tried her best to breathe through the sudden nausea. "Why are you making me watch this?" she gasped through gritted teeth. Her stomach heaved again.

"This is not the only thing you need to see, but you must understand the pain of battle," the spirit replied. "Follow me, Freya. We need to find the Goblin Queen. Although, at this time, we all knew her as the Winter Princess."

It was a new name for the same face. Freya didn't care what they had called the woman. All she cared about was the way to defeat her.

Freya allowed the spirit to drag her across the battlefield. Her senses shifted, the living realm colliding with the world of the dead. She could see the people as they were when they battled, but also feel their bones crunching beneath her feet.

Her stomach clenched again, but she refused to allow the gorge to spew out of her mouth. She couldn't throw up. She was stronger than this.

So she walked through the battlefield with her head held high. Even though she was terrified of all the things she saw along the way.

A goblin with the head of an owl wielded a sword nearly as long as it was tall. That sword took out so many fae who couldn't get anywhere near the owl headed woman. Until an archer without a face caught her in the throat with a gold fletched arrow.

Scenes like that played out before her in the hundreds as so many people lost their lives. Until they got to the very heart of the battle where a small tent stood.

"What is this place?" she asked.

"The spirit realm exists in the now, the then, and the time in between," the cloaked ghost said. "While these spirits battle, this was what happened the night before. Here you will discover all that you need to know."

She approached the tent and reached her arm toward the swaying curtain. But at the last second, she looked back at the ghost. "This is the moment that will convince me to kill her?"

The hood shifted to the side, and she saw for a second what the ghost had been. A handsome goblin man, with the face of a brown tabby cat, and the paws to match. He'd once been very handsome, and yet, now he was nothing more than a spirit.

He moved again, and the visage of what he had once been disappeared. "No, Freya. You need no more justification to take a life. There is never a good reason to do so. What you are about to witness will show you the truth. She didn't become evil. She wasn't always bad. But she still made choices that would give her power. Now you will know where that came from, and such knowledge should be used wisely."

A gust of wind blew him out of existence, leaving her with a thousand unanswered questions. Frowning, she turned back to the ghostly tent. This would explain it all? She didn't know what she might find the Winter Princess doing, but she supposed the only way to find out was to pull back the curtain and step into the past.

Freya stepped into the tent and eyed the three figures around a large table in the center. They weren't ghosts like the others. The interior of the tent was bright with color and vibrant with life. This was a memory, not just the remains of the faeries who were left here.

The Goblin Queen looked different back then. She wore silver armor that appeared more pretty than functional. Freya had thought the Winter Princess would be more likely to wear something aggressive. Instead, her blue skirts were heavier than normal. Her hair was left unbound and wild around her face. In youth, the Winter Princess had been a lovely, delicate thing. Not the hard edged woman who was apt to kill her servants.

Two men stood beside her. One tall and white haired, too similar in appearance to be anyone other than the King of the Winter Court. He wore a crown atop his silver head and a finely made blue suit with silver embroidered edges. The other man was entirely clad in armor, including a silver helm that hid his face.

The Winter Princess pointed to a map on the table. "We should attack them here."

Her father shook his head. "No, daughter. That would leave Eldridge alone with his force. And then we will lose them all. I taught you better than that."

"Precisely. You did teach me better." The Winter Princess looked to the man in armor and then blinked. Her father froze in place, as though time had stopped. Then she said, "Did you get everything in place?"

"Yes. Eldridge will assume we made a grave error in choosing to attack this section of the battlefield. The Summer Lord has agreed to capture him on one condition." The guard widened his stance, as though he were afraid to tell her what the Summer Lord wanted. "He wishes for the promise of your hand if he succeeds."

The Winter Princess snorted. "I will have no husband, but if this succeeds then I will be able to destroy the Summer Lord once and for all. With the Goblin throne, the powers of the Winter Court, and Eldridge at my side, I will have so much power that no one will ever question me again."

"How exactly are you going to take his power from him?" The guard tilted his head to the side, then moved to the other side of the table. He watched the Winter Princess intensely.

Freya thought maybe he was in love with her. The Winter Princess brought that sort of attention to herself. Her story was one of many unrequited loves, her own and others.

The woman who would become the Goblin Queen tilted her

head back and laughed. "My dear. Magic is easy to syphon off of anyone that I desire. A little pain can go a very long way."

"You would harm him? I thought you wanted him for yourself."

The Winter Princess stared back down at the battlefield map, and her lips curved into a dangerously dark smile. "I did. I do. But he will come to me of his own accord, because he wishes to be with me. If that is only to end his torture, then so be it. He will desire me. No matter how long that takes for me to convince him."

Freya's stomach rolled again. So that was the plan this whole time? The Goblin Queen was stealing his magic, as they had thought, but she also wanted to torment him until he finally caved? That wasn't finding a lover.

It was creating a slave.

She didn't need to watch any more of this madness. Stumbling out of the tent, she fell onto her hands and knees in the ash. A pang of pain rocked through her entire being. As though someone had shoved a knife in between her ribs.

Sucking in a deep breath, she pressed her hand to what she was certain would be a mortal wound. Except, there was nothing there when she pulled her fingers back.

Another blast of pain echoed through her head. Crying out, she cupped her skull in her hands and rocked back and forth until the ache disappeared.

What had just happened? She'd felt pain before from Eldridge trying to reach out, but never like that.

Gasping in air, she forced herself to stand again. She had to get moving. She had to get the knife and then... then what? She had no idea.

The hooded ghost materialized before her. He'd pushed his hood back this time, letting her see the strange skull beneath it. Fanged teeth clacked as he spoke. "The Queen is taking what she needs from Eldridge. But that doesn't mean she cannot be beaten."

"Her servant said there was a knife that could take her life," Freya replied.

Her head still felt like it was splitting open. The pain made her vision skew to the side. Why was this happening now? What could cause pain like this?

She had to know. And this figure before her was the only one who might be able to explain.

"My head," she started, pointing to her temples. "It's throbbing in a way I've never felt before. It's only hurt like this when Eldridge has been trying to contact me, but I don't see him. Why is my head hurting?"

The ghost looked through her for a moment, his attention diverting somewhere she couldn't follow. Finally, the skull tilted back and paid attention to the mortal standing before him. "The Queen knows you're up to something. She's realized you're not there, and that means something horrible could happen after all. You need to hurry, Freya. The King needs you."

She was trying to hurry. But no one else seemed to be in the same rush. "I need to find the knife before I go anywhere. I've come all this way just to find it, and if I return empty handed, then all of this will be for nothing."

The ghost lurched forward, reached for her, and grabbed her by the collar of her jacket. It dragged her closer until she was staring into the bottomless pits of its eyes. "Will you kill her? I need to know if you can actually do it."

She gasped and held onto the skeletal wrists. "Yes!" Freya struggled to free herself from the grip, but couldn't wiggle herself free. "Yes, I can do it if I have to."

"And you will have to, Freya of Woolwich." The ghost released her and retreated.

He reached into the folds of his cloak and pulled out an ice blue knife. It was made in the old ways. A metal handle with leather wrapped around it for a grip. The blade itself was made by chipping away the edges of the ice so it was sharpened by brute force alone.

This was not a weapon to hold with finesse. This was meant to kill.

The ghost held it out for her to take. "Wield this wisely. Save our king and stop all the horrors that this Queen desires to commit."

Freya took the blade and hissed as a bitter chill seeped through the thick wool of her mittens. The cold was white hot, enough to freeze her fingers off if she wasn't careful. She wrapped it in the edge of her jacket, up and around, until she could tuck the entire thing into the jacket's pocket. That side of her body would be colder, but at least she wouldn't get frostbite from the enchanted blade.

"Thank you," she said. "I will make sure that she doesn't do what you all fear. I will stop her."

"I hope you will." The ghost turned away from her and lifted its hood. "The king believes in you, and he doesn't give that regard lightly. Now, he needs you more than ever, Freya. Save him and defeat the Queen."

"How am I going to get back fast enough?" She stumbled after the ghost. "I don't even know where he is."

The spirit lifted a thin hand and pointed to the rotting reindeer. "Take your steed, Hero."

She supposed she'd done stranger things in her life than ride the spirit of a reindeer. Freya hurried to the beast, reached up, and used the horns to haul herself onto its back. "The beast knows where to go?"

The edges of the spirit were already wispy as it disappeared into the fog. "Yes. Trust in the magic. It will take you where you are needed most."

CHAPTER 20

Freya held onto the reindeer's antlers for dear life. They practically flew away from that haunted battlefield with the thousands of ghosts who remained behind. The beast's sides heaved as they thundered across the land and ran headlong into the blizzard that surrounded the Goblin Queen's palace.

The reindeer never faltered, even when they struck the side of the storm with all the force of a battering ram. Icy shards of snow blasted Freya's face, tearing at her sensitive skin in tiny daggers. Bits of the reindeer fell off with the sheer force of the wind.

Still, they went forward.

Sides heaving, the reindeer moved faster when a blast of icy air tried to force them back. It tucked its head, forcing Freya to press herself lengthwise against its back. They rode with a ferocity that she hadn't known a beast like this still had in it. She would have assumed the great beast had fought its final battle long ago.

But then again, this was the steed of a goblin warrior. Of course, the creature knew how to continue forward when something was driving it back.

She tried to reach out to the Goblin King in her mind, but he did not respond. She whispered endearments in the hopes he would answer. "Eldridge," she called out. "You have to wake up. You have to talk to me."

No one responded.

Freya realized with horror that she was more clear-headed than she had been since Eldridge started reaching out through her mind. She just hadn't realized how foggy her reality had become. She'd gotten used to dealing with the ache behind her eyes. The strange feeling of floating had just been because she was in the faerie realms. Not that he was dipping into her perception and altering the reality that she saw.

Now, she wondered how long the Goblin King had been meddling with her head.

The snow made it impossible to see what direction the reindeer was running. She didn't know if they were heading back toward the castle, or if they were going somewhere else. Freya could only pray this faerie ghost was taking her where she needed to go. And that was away from the Goblin Queen's castle.

If Eldridge had been in the castle, she would have found him by now. Wouldn't she have?

After all, she had pawed through more of those rooms than she could count. And no matter how hard she tried to snoop through the Goblin Queen's home, one thing had been very clear. No one other than the Goblin Queen was awake.

Other than those two strange faeries who had brought her to the castle. The faeries who had been sent to the very outer reaches of this land to watch for intruders.

Or at least, that's what Freya assumed they had been sent out there for.

Maybe she knew nothing in this story. Maybe there was so much more yet to be revealed.

The reindeer tossed its head and the thundering hoofbeats slowed. Though the storm still blasted overhead, she could almost feel the reindeer's intent to stop. It wasn't going to continue for much longer, which meant they had to be near something important. Didn't they?

With the thought came a frigid blast of wind. And then, appearing out of thin air, an ominous prison emerged from the fog.

It was tall and dark, as though the ice that made up the sharp edges was so deep and thick that it had turned black. No light could penetrate the tall, jagged structure that rose into the air like daggers being thrust at the sky. They created a strange pattern around the open archway that led into the prison. Perhaps like a snowflake, if they could look that ominous and threatening.

Swallowing hard, she gripped the reindeer's last remaining fur as it trotted up to the archway and then stopped.

"This is the place she's keeping the Goblin King?" she asked. Her voice wavered with dread.

The reindeer tossed its head, almost as though it were saying yes, this is the place.

Suddenly, Freya second guessed coming here on her own. And though she still had the magical dagger clutched in her fist, she worried that it would do nothing to stop whatever beast lurked in those darkened doors.

What if the Goblin Queen had some kind of guard in the prison? What if she was supposed to battle off some great wyrm like the carving on the throne room doors?

The reindeer didn't give her an option to fear any longer. It reared up, tossing her from its back without a second thought. Freya tumbled through the air, then struck the ice and snow hard. Breath wheezed from her lungs while the ghostly beast disappeared. Fading from view as though it had never been there at all.

"Thank you for the help," she said. The wind caught her voice and dashed it away. She could only hope it somehow found the spirits who had helped her find the Goblin King.

Getting back onto her feet, Freya swept the snow from her skirts and the long edge of her jacket. She patted the knife where it was still in her pocket, releasing her grip on the hilt that was the only comforting thing in this realm thus far. She should have known this wouldn't be easy.

And yet, the sight of this prison was enough to make the hairs on her arms stand up. It loomed above her, eerily silent even though she knew there should have been some kind of sound.

Where were the guards?

Where was the beast that would prevent people from walking in without permission?

Freya had more questions than that, but those two were the ones that stuck in her mind. The Goblin Queen was no fool. Surely she would put Eldridge in a cage guarded by a hundred men. All armed to the teeth and ready to battle at a moment's notice.

Unless...

No, it couldn't be true. But the facts were laid out before her as she stepped into the mouth of the cavern that was the Goblin Queen's prison.

There were no guards here. Because the Goblin Queen had believed no one could find this place.

Because no one else was awake.

Yet again, a faerie had underestimated Freya. She walked into the prison without a single person telling her to stop. Her footsteps echoed inside the main cavern, the only sound in the entire building.

There obviously should have been guards. Armor still hung on the walls, and it looked as though someone had painted scenes of battle behind them. Although the ice distorted the paintings now, warping the warriors even more than their faerie bodies already were.

Doors led off in all different directions, though there were no iron bars on them, so Freya had no idea which way each door led.

The long line of doors continued down through the hall until it disappeared into the darkness at the end.

Benches lined the walls, likely for guards to take a rest while they were guarding those the Winter Palace wanted to lock away.

There should have been people here. A lot of people. And yet, this ancient cavern was filled only with the ghosts of prisoners who had lost their lives in this place.

Gulping, Freya pushed open the first door on her left. There was no one within the prison cell. The icy magic of the Goblin Queen filled it to the brim. The walls were made of ice, white and blue light slashing through in intervals that made her immediately nauseous. Over and over, the light pulsed. The strange pattern was disorienting and horrible.

Maybe that was the point.

She pushed open another door and saw this one was completely black. The ice was so thick that she wondered if it was even ice anymore. It looked like stone.

The third room was filled with a thin layer of ice and water in between the walls. This one also made her feel ill, but mostly because of the strange fish that stared at her when she entered. They hovered inside the walls, their mouths full of sharp teeth and a bright light hung from their heads. Obviously, these creatures were starving, and they wanted a piece of her flesh to feast upon.

Freya closed that door with a solid thump and continued her way down the hall.

She might have kept going forever if one of the doors hadn't hidden an occupant behind it. She paused and stared at a faerie who looked very familiar. It was the big faerie who had first found her when they entered the Winter Court. The faerie who now sat on the floor, tears dripping down his cheeks, with a pile of ruby red ice stacked next to him.

Was that the birch faerie?

She could only imagine it was. The pieces of that faerie's

body were hard to forget. The sharp edges had faded a bit, likely from the big faerie touching them so much. A stacked pile of ice stood before him, little pieces of what had once been his friend carefully stuck to each other in the hopes that he might put the other faerie back together.

Freya stepped into the room. Her heart squeezed for this poor man who had only wanted to help his friend. The one who had wanted to impress his Queen, only to fail in the worst way imaginable.

She cleared her throat. "Excuse me? Do you think putting him back together will bring him back?"

The big faerie looked over his shoulder, large brown eyes filled with tears. "The Queen said I had to do this, mortal. I don't know if this will bring him back, or if it's just another of her punishments. I hope it does. You see..." He reached forward and touched a hand to what had once been the other faerie's knee. "He was my dearest friend. My oldest friend. We were born at the exact same time, and our mother's always said that meant we were supposed to look after each other."

Carefully stepping around the pieces of the birch faerie's body, she crouched down beside the living one. Freya stared at the work he had completed thus far. It was an impressive amount of pieces, and the big faerie had put quite a few of them together in a manner that made sense. The frozen creature was looking more like himself.

"I need to find the Goblin King," she muttered. "You know that, but now I think you know why as well."

"You want to defeat the Goblin Queen." He nodded, then picked up another ruby red piece. "I don't think you'll succeed. You've seen what she can do. Why would you even try?"

She pondered the question, because it was a hard one. Freya could give him the normal, heroic speech that anyone else might have provided. She could tell him that she was trying to right her own wrongs, save her own soul, bring back order to the courts and become a legend to the faeries.

Instead, she decided to tell him the truth. "Because it's the right thing to do," she replied. "Someone has to try."

Ever so carefully, she reached out and touched the very edge of the frozen faerie. Even though he had terrified her in life, he still deserved to live. All faeries terrified her. That didn't mean they should die.

The big faerie nodded again, his eyes watching her hands with rapt attention. As if he thought she might hurt his friend.

When she did no such thing, he heaved a great sigh. "Your Goblin King is in the very last cell, if that's what you're looking for. But I don't think he's going to be much help."

"Why's that?"

"I think he might be dead."

The words zinged through her as though she'd been struck by lightning. Dead? No. The Goblin King couldn't die. He was far too stubborn for that, and he was the type to wait for her just so he could laugh that she had worried about him.

He couldn't be dead.

Her heart beating out of her chest, she stood and raced to the door. "I hope you get your friend back together!" she shouted over her shoulder as she raced away.

The hall turned dark and ominous. She put her hand on the wall to guide herself as she continued running. It didn't matter if something on the floor tripped her. She'd get back up so she could find the Goblin King faster.

Genuine fear made her breath catch in her throat and her hands shake. What if he really was dead? What if she was too late?

Freya struck the wall at the end of the tunnel hard. Her forehead bounced off the ice, leaving her dazed as pain scattered her thoughts. Though the pain was familiar, considering how often her head ached these days.

She'd give her left arm for that headache back if it meant that Eldridge was still alive.

Shifting to her right, she opened the first door and prayed it was his cell. It wasn't. This one was empty just like the others, black and devoid of life. Spinning on her heel, she reached for the other cell and threw it open with a resounding crack as it struck the wall.

This cell differed from the others.

The walls, ceiling, and floor were composed entirely of crystals. Jagged edged and sharp, they glowed with a dull purple light. Freya had only seen such crystals once in her life, and they had been in her mother's study. Amethyst pillars were supposed to help calm a person's mind.

Obviously, that was not the intent of these. The sharp edges were like daggers. The points were clearly meant to be spears, thrown into the skin of any person who dared to step into those awful, horrible rooms.

At the very back of the cell was a lean, dark form. Crumpled against the floor where streaks of blood turned the crystal pillars red.

The Goblin King had been forced to lie upon the floor at some point. Harsh wounds on his sides turned his white shirt blood red. Strips of his skin laid against his sides, only made worse by a sudden shiver that rocked through his body.

All the tension blasted from her lungs and her shoulders slumped forward. He was alive.

Thank all the gods and the faerie worshipped beings that the Goblin King was alive.

CHAPTER 21

Freya was suddenly very glad for her sturdy boots. The sharp edges of the crystals dug through the thick soles of her shoes, though they never quite reached her feet. They tried their best, though. A dark magic filled these rocks with a lust for pain and anguish. It seemed that they almost whispered with the screams of all those they had harmed in the past.

The Goblin King's shivers only drove the crystals deeper into his skin. The bright blossoms of color on his shirt were spreading too fast. Every time he shifted, she could see the crystals dig deeper into him, like roots tangling through the earth. He was wedging himself into the painful spikes and she didn't think he even realized it.

And she could see a thousand cuts all over his skin. Some were shallow, like on his hand that appeared over his shoulder, his fingers curling as though he were trying to hug himself. Some were very deep, like the ones she could now see on his thighs. Each a perfect puncture wound in the shape of a crystal.

Soon, she would get him out of here. He just had to make it a few more minutes and then they would be free.

Finally.

She crouched beside him and reached out a hand. "Eldridge?" she whispered. "It's me."

He rolled at the sound of her voice. She could hear the wet suction of crystals coming out of his skin, then sliding back into wounds they had already created in his back. His eyes searched for her, but those dark, lovely, silver eyes were fogged over with a thick layer of film. One was so bruised around the socket, she could only imagine someone had tried to take the orb out.

"Freya?" he muttered, his voice weak and thready. "I know you can't really be there. I'm too weak to reach you. What spell is the Goblin Queen sending to torment me now?"

Tears built in her eyes and spilled down her cheeks. The warm droplets fell onto his face, sizzling where they struck because his skin was so cold. "It's me, Eldridge. I'm really here. Didn't I tell you that I would find you? All you had to do was wait for me."

He lifted a hand, though the movement was obviously painful. He touched the tips of his claws to her cheekbone, his hands shaking. The soft, sad smile on his face made her heart bleed.

His voice was still strong, though. "Oh, my darling hero. You aren't here at all, because the Queen has had her way with you. We failed, don't you know? Perhaps she sent your spirit to me."

"I'm no more a ghost than the giant in that cave. I haven't joined the creatures on that battlefield and neither will you." Freya leaned down, peering at the crystals still lodged in his back. "We have to get you out of here. But I don't know if I can lift you."

He apparently wasn't listening to her at all. Eldridge stared up into the ceiling and let out a half hearted, sad, chuckle. "You know, no one's ever beaten me before. I think that was why I was so fascinated with you. Obsessed, really."

She tried to wiggle her fingers underneath him, but the crystals created a wall of sharp edges. She would have to haul him up, yanking the crystals out of his back in the process. And though that sounded painful, there was no other option. "Yes, well you helped me defeat you, you know."

"Not really." He moved one of his shoulders, wincing. Although his reaction was more one of discomfort rather than absolute agony. "You would have done it without my help, it just would have taken you a little longer. That's why I was helping. Just to see if I could get you to do it faster with a little help."

"I still would have failed in the Spring Maiden's court. I would still be asleep if you hadn't gotten me out of there." She picked up his hands and gripped them tight. "Eldridge, I'm going to pull you up very quickly. It's going to hurt, I imagine. I need you to stay quiet, because we don't know if someone will hear."

He frowned, then tugged her closer to him. He used her hands as leverage, yanking her to his face that she almost fell down onto the crystals herself. "I need you to understand this, Freya. I was interested in you. Not because you beat me, but because you are one of the most fascinating women I have ever met. And if I could have kissed you a thousand times in your lifetime, I would have. I should have."

"We don't have time for this, Eldridge."

"There is always time for romance." He smiled and some of the fog cleared from his eyes. Just a bit, as he ran his claws through the dark locks of her hair. "There will always be time for us, no matter how many armies stand in my way."

She took a deep breath and decided to rip at the wound. She needed him to focus on the now, and not whatever drivel he was spitting.

Even if it did make her heart flutter.

"There is no us, Eldridge. There is only what is happening currently and what has to happen later. And right now, I need you to get up so we can get you out of this room."

He frowned again, those delicious little lines appearing between his eyes. "I'm trying to tell you that I'm falling in love with you, you ridiculous woman. And yet, you refuse to listen to what I have to say?"

"Yes, I will listen to whatever you want when we get out of this horrible palace and this disgusting Queen's clutches, but I won't listen to another thing for a moment further." Even though she lost all the air in her lungs at the word love.

He couldn't love her.

They hadn't known each other very long, and in that amount of time they had fought against each other, and then he'd been stuck in a prison. He was merely saying the words because he could very well die alone in this cold, painful place.

That was the only reason. Definitely not because he had these feelings for her that he just couldn't shake. She refused to believe it.

If she did, then she would have to admit her own obsessive thoughts were the same thing. That she was falling in love with the Goblin King and that meant everything had to change. Everything.

So instead, she shook her head and drew away from him. "Eldridge, we have to go now. I need you to stand up."

He was still ignoring her. Willfully staying in that floating place where he didn't have to feel this pain or realize that he was about to get out of his prison.

Freya stood up and braced her legs on either side of his prone body. She would have to do this with one harsh tug, but it shouldn't be as difficult as she had originally thought. He'd lost a lot of weight since the last time she'd seen him, and he was always on the thinner side.

In contrast, she'd likely gained weight. All this walking and running and doing gods know what in this place had packed on the muscle. She looked more like the Viking women her mother used to idealize than a noble.

Good. She'd rather be terrifying than beautiful.

Freya grasped his hands again and tried to warn him one last time. "This is really going to hurt Eldridge. Don't scream. Neither of us know if she decided guards weren't necessary or if they just happen to not be here right now, all right?"

He stared up at her with a bright smile on his face. "You are beautiful. I'm glad you'll be the last thing I see."

"Idiot," she muttered.

They might as well get this over with. He was going to scream and if she had to haul him out of the prison herself, then this would take more time than they had. So they couldn't afford to wait any longer.

With a great heave, she used her legs as leverage and yanked him out of the crystals. The wet sound that echoed through the room made her stomach lurch. She couldn't throw up. Not now, but damned if she didn't feel the acidic vomit pressing against the back of her throat.

Eldridge too made a horrible sound. A cross between a moan and a groan, he collapsed into her arms with a ragged wheeze.

Freya struggled to hold on to him, blood slicking her palms and making it incredibly difficult to hang onto him. Why was he so skinny? Damn it, she needed something to hold on to that wasn't just wound covered bones, but that was all his form was at this point.

"Eldridge," she grunted. "Wake up. I need you to stand on your own, I don't think I can carry you out of here."

"Trying," he weakly muttered in her ear. "I can't... I can't feel my legs. Am I doing it?"

Not even close. He was still limp, hanging off her like she was lifting a corpse.

This would get easier, she reminded herself. He would be able to stand up on his own, just not right now. And maybe it was the room. Maybe this cave was part of how the Goblin Queen stole his magic.

If Freya got him out of this prison cell, then he might be stronger, gain his own power back. Or, at the very least, she could set him down on one of those benches and then they could figure out their next steps.

Freya wished the reindeer hadn't taken off. She could really use that beast at the moment.

But she could do this. She could lift him up and prove herself to be stronger than any of the faeries' had thought she was. Freya leaned down, hooked her arm between his legs, and draped him across her back.

Step by agonizing step, she made her way across the crystals. They sank into her boots, digging through the leather and reaching for her feet. By the time she made it halfway to the doors, they succeeded in what their dark magic desperately wanted. Every step dug deeper into her heels, blistering pain rocking through the bones of her feet and into her very soul. She left thick, bloody footsteps in her wake.

The magic threaded through her mind, and then she understood why the Goblin King had thought she wasn't real. The magic in the crystals was a kind of poison that dug not only into the flesh but also into the mind.

"Freya!" Her sister lunged into view with her arms outstretched. "You can't take him out of the cell. He will die!"

She gritted her teeth and took another step. "No, he won't. He'll die if he stays in this cell."

"You have to listen to me. You're about to make a very grievous mistake. We can't afford to lose all this time. If you don't leave him in this cell, then he will die and everything will be for nothing."

"No," she snarled. "And you aren't my sister. Go away."

The image of Esther faded from view, only for the birch faerie to appear in front of the door. His entire body was cracked, as if the big faerie had finished, but he hadn't healed. Instead, his form had become a mosaic of flesh and bone. "You aren't going anywhere, little girl."

"Yes, I am." Freya took two more steps, then paused to catch her breath. "And you're going to move."

"I'm going to use your name against you. I'm going to whisper it into a curse that makes you take this visage on." He waved a hand up and down his body. "You're going to become me."

"Well, that's a cute threat, but it's not going to happen." She blew a breath at the hair that had fallen in front of her face. "You can keep trying to threaten me, but nothing is going to change. I'm taking him out of this cavern, no matter how many of you try to stop me. You're just figments of my imagination."

The Goblin Queen waved a hand through the birch faerie and he disappeared. But the Queen stood there with a grin on her face. "Am I, Freya? Or did you just walk into the trap I laid out for you?"

Freya froze. Was she really here? Or was this just another part of the poison that wanted to drag both her and Goblin King back into the crystal spikes?

No one knew Freya was here. The big faerie wouldn't have told the Queen... Would he?

In her brief hesitation, she could hear the cackling laughter from within the crystals. They had stopped her. And whether the Queen was real or not, she was going to stay in this cell because she didn't want to fight against the Goblin Queen.

The vision of the Queen put her hand on the door to the cell. "You're going to stay in here with him, if you want him so badly. But nothing that you do, little girl, is going to slow what I have planned. I will become the greatest Goblin Queen to ever live, and a mere mortal has no chance of defeating me. Even with the Goblin King at her side."

She refused to believe that was true. Because even if she got out of here, even if the Goblin Queen wasn't real, then she was still going to fight this woman. She still had the crystal dagger in her pocket.

If now was the time for her to kill the Goblin Queen, then why was she wasting any more breaths?

Freya took another step forward. Then another. "You are not going to stop me. No one is going to stop me, no matter how hard you try. He's not staying in here a moment longer."

She stood directly in front of the Queen and glared up at her.

Freya still didn't know if this woman was a mirage or if she was really there. But the Queen would step aside, regardless.

The Queen looked her up and down, then sneered. "I'm going to lock you up in here for the rest of time, little mortal."

"No," she replied. "You aren't."

Freya stepped through the vision and into the hallway beyond the crystal cell. Immediately, all the weight that had been tugging her backward, the magic that wanted to do her harm, fell away. Eldridge even felt lighter on her shoulders, as if much of the weight pressing down upon her had actually been from the magic. Not him.

Now she could breathe. Now, she could release all the tension that had been riding on her shoulders and she could take a deep breath.

Gently, Freya shifted the Goblin King down onto one of the nearby benches. He flopped a little, but shook himself when she got him seated. Eldridge put out a hand and braced himself on the stone.

He blinked rapidly, and with each fluttering movement, the fog over his eyes cleared.

"Freya?" he asked, reaching for her. He caught a lock of her hair between his fingers, gently moving it back and forth as though he couldn't believe the texture. "You were really in that horrible cell with me?"

"Yes, I was." She slapped his hand. "Stop doing that. Of course I was in the room with you. I said I would get you out, didn't I?"

He let his hand fall back to his side. "You did. I'm afraid I wasn't all that optimistic at the end there."

"Oh, you know better than that," she said with a laugh. "How many times have I surprised you, Goblin King?"

He reached for her again, drawing her down onto the bench with him. "I thought I told you to stop calling me that? You know my name, Freya. Use it."

The heat from his mouth tempted her greatly. She wanted to

press her lips to his. To feel that heat that always spread through her body the moment he kissed her. The warmth that only Eldridge could seem to bring.

"Eldridge," she whispered, knowing he could feel her breath. "You had to know I was coming for you. You had to know that after all this time, I wouldn't let you suffer alone."

"I did," he replied. "I made an error in forgetting that you are the hero of this story, Freya of Woolwich. However, could I make that up to you?"

"I can think of a few ways."

She leaned forward and pressed her lips to his. The soft, plush comfort of his mouth hadn't changed in all the time that he'd been stuck in his cell. He was still passion incarnate, tasting of apple pie and sweet treats.

Eldridge slid his hand to the back of her neck, drawing her closer. He dipped into her mouth with tongue and lips, devouring her whole as though she was the only water and he was a dying man in a desert.

Perhaps he was. Perhaps he found some nirvana in her kiss because he didn't act as though he'd been wounded, or even as though he had been in a cell at all.

Eldridge took. He feasted. And when he finally pulled back for air, Freya gasped in a breath of shock. Her stomach clenched in desire and her heart raced in her chest, pounding against her ribs as though the organ itself wanted to be touched by him.

The Goblin King dragged the back of his hand across his lips, the fire in his eyes so bright it burned her very soul. "I've been waiting to do that again for a very long time."

She sucked in a long, shuddering breath. "Was now really the right time for it?"

"There's no right time for romance," he repeated with a wink. "Or had you already forgotten that so quickly?"

"Right." She took a step away from him, clearing her throat. "You did say that, didn't you?"

He nodded. The grin on his face was a little too prideful for her taste. "You said you had the dagger."

"I do." Back to business as usual, apparently, as though nothing had happened between them. She didn't know if she should be relieved, or if it should sting a little. "I still don't know what to do with it, but I have the dagger."

"It's the first step. The second is getting me out of these bloody clothes and back into something a little more... intimidating." He smoothed a hand down his chest, wincing when his fingers bumped over wounds. "And perhaps a bath."

Another voice interrupted them. The big faerie boomed down the hall, "I can get you back into the castle, if that would help."

Eldridge lifted a brow, then called back, "It would, friend!"

Freya met Eldridge's questioning stare with a shrug. "I don't know, he seems like he hates the Queen as much as we do by now. I think we can probably trust him."

"Then let's get back into the castle." Eldridge started toward the voice. Each step was an exaggerated limp, but at least he was walking on his own.

Freya rushed to his side and tucked herself under his arm. At the very least, Eldridge had someone to help him now. And that was a start.

CHAPTER 22

They snuck through the castle halls, a little slower than Freya would have liked, but at least no one knew they were there. The big faerie left them at the hidden entrance with a nod and a sharp-edged smile. "Kill the bitch for me, would you?"

Freya didn't know if that meant he was supporting them, or something worse. He could ruin this all for them if he decided to get involved. But she didn't want to kill anyone and still had a small amount of hope that she wouldn't have to. Unfortunately, her reality was setting in.

As she helped Eldridge limp down the hall toward her private quarters, she had to come to terms with the reality that she was going to have to kill the Queen. The dagger burned a hole in her pocket, poking at her with its sharp edges and reminding her that she was, without a doubt, the hero of this story. Which meant she was also going to hold all the guilt herself.

They made it to her room without anyone seeing them. She shoved it open and helped push Eldridge through, then slammed it shut behind them before any ice creature realized they were back.

She wanted a few minutes with the Goblin King to herself.

Then, all of his subjects could come rushing in and ask him whatever questions they might have. And she understood their desire to see him. He was their king. And the only good one they'd had in a while. Arrow, at the very least, had every right to see that Eldridge was healthy and whole.

But for a few moments, just a few, she wanted to pretend that it was just the two of them.

They hadn't gotten such a respite before, and Freya wanted to know what would happen if they did. If she was alone with him for more than a few moments, with no rush to save someone else, what would happen?

Her heart raced as she turned around and pressed her back to the door. Eldridge was standing near the frozen fireplace, staring down at it with a frown.

He was a picture of strength, even bloody and broken as he was. A king returning to a castle where he found only disappointment and changes. Perhaps, in other circumstances, he might have been glad to return to this castle where he'd spent some of his formative years. Instead, he looked saddened by everything he saw.

Eldridge cleared his throat. "You know, this used to be the most beautiful palace in all the courts. Winter was known as the place for artists to gather when they wanted to be inspired. I met so many people here who had more talent, more heart, than any people I've met since. The art this place influenced would have made even the most hardened of hearts weep."

She could imagine it was so. The few pieces she'd seen here were immaculate. "What was it like when you lived here?"

He chuckled. "It was more than this. More than some icy, snowy room where so few people could ever survive. It was warm and wonderful and so filled with hope. Before the wars. Before... Well. Before I did what I had to do."

"Do you really believe that?" She took a step closer, holding herself in check so she didn't launch herself at his back. "It doesn't sound like you believe you did what you had to do."

"You can't deny my part in all this. I have spent a large portion of my life trying to make amends for all the pain I wrought here, but nothing I do seems to matter." He turned away from the fireplace, staring into her eyes as though she held the answer to something. Like she could heal him. "I don't think you understand, Freya. I froze them all into mere sculptures of themselves. They were incapable of movement. Of dreaming. Of doing anything other than remain exactly where I put them because that was the only way I knew how to stop her."

"And you were right to stop her," she replied. Freya took a step closer, lifted her hands, and pressed them to his heart. "If you hadn't done what you needed to do, then she would have done all this sooner. She hasn't even woken up the Winter Court. Just those two faeries who she sent out into the middle of nowhere to watch for someone who might end up in the kingdom. She doesn't care about the Winter Court. She just cares about herself."

"Yet, I haven't stopped her again." His hands moved as if by their own accord. Eldridge slid his fingers into the soft dips above her hips, drawing her closer into his arms with a long sigh. "This place was beautiful before her. I miss it. Just as you must miss your home."

She did, but not as much as he might think.

Freya tilted her head back and stared into his eyes. "I miss my home because of the warmth that it brought my soul, but I don't miss the place. I miss the feelings that came with it."

Some of the tension in Eldridge's thin shoulders eased. "Yes, I suppose you're right. There wasn't much here for me in the long run. Just a family who had always wanted a son, and a sister who thought I would give her the world on a silver platter. I failed them all, in the end. And maybe that's why I feel so guilty being here."

Freya didn't know how to tell him that the Goblin Queen was actually in love with him. That was a bridge they would need to cross. But how did one say that his sister was in love with him? The words felt twisted on her tongue. So wrong that it was impossible to believe they were true.

And yet, they didn't share blood. Could she blame the Goblin Queen, when she herself was falling for the same man?

"Eldridge..." She licked her lips and figured it was better to tell him now rather than later. "I think you need to know something. The Goblin Queen, she's not doing all this just because she wants power."

"I know." He nodded, the fog returning to his eyes for a moment before clearing. "Do you think I didn't know all those years ago? Even when we were children, she wanted us to be something more. She wanted a life that couldn't happen. And though she tried to force that life to take form, it wouldn't. To live like that, in constant frustration and disappointment, turns a person into something twisted and ugly."

Freya flinched back from the words. She didn't know what she would do if he had called her ugly. And not physically. She knew the Goblin King meant the Winter Princess had always been an ugly person deep in her very being.

The words were cruel.

But they were truthful.

Freya cleared her throat and nodded. "Well, then. As long as you are aware of that."

"I need to clean this blood off me. And I'm afraid I must ask you to uphold a promise you said to me a while ago."

"Which is?" She didn't remember all the things she'd said, but a promise? Freya wasn't certain she had ever offered such a thing. Although, he would remember better than she supposed.

He drew her even closer, tucking her underneath his chin and pressing his lips to the top of her head. "You offered some of your own energy. That I could take some of it to use magic again. Is that still something you'd feel comfortable with?"

Freya didn't have the faintest idea what that would entail. He would take some of her own life and then transfer that into magic? Would that mean she would be weaker, or would it feel like she was ill?

Anything was a risk she was willing to take. The Goblin King was a much stronger person than she was, and far more useful in their fight against the Queen. He knew the Goblin Queen better than anyone else, and he needed to be prepared for anything she threw their way.

So she nodded. "All right. If it would help you, then yes. Please take whatever you need and we'll see what happens."

"You won't feel a thing," he whispered into her ear. "I promise. You know I would never hurt you."

Of course he wouldn't, at least not on purpose. Freya let him take a little more of her weight and then sighed. "Tell me a story about when you were younger, then. Just to keep me distracted."

He chuckled. "You make it sound as though you'll need me to. There will be no pain, Freya. You won't even feel it."

"You don't know that," she argued. "Neither do I."

"I know you won't. I've done this before." He tightened his arms around her waist, and she felt the slightest tug in her belly.

It was a faint feeling, like a butterfly was playing through her torso. Not quite anxiety, but certainly not comfortable either. Blowing out a long, relaxing breath, she tried very hard not to focus on the sensation of her own magic leaking out of her body.

Magic. As if mortals even had any.

"When I first came here, there was a single person who entertained me more than anyone else. It was a little boy by the name of Hugo. He was a very small child, more pixie like than one of the fae in the Winter Court. I never really thought much of him other than the slip of a boy was cute. He used to play pranks on anyone he could get his hands on." Eldridge tightened his grip around her waist. "You reminded me of him when I first saw you."

Freya scoffed. "As if. I was never a prankster, and I certainly wouldn't have been interested at that age. I was much too serious."

"So was he. Until he wasn't anymore and then suddenly, it was like all the chains had come off him. He wanted to live more than he wanted to see life pass him by." He combed his fingers through her hair, tugging on the strands and playing with the ends as he always did. "I saw you and I wondered what would be the thing that makes you realize you needed to live."

"What was it that made this little boy want to live?" She shifted her hands around his waist, holding onto him even though it must have caused him great pain.

His wounds were underneath her hands. The ragged edges of flesh pressed against her fingertips and she wanted to go back in time so that he would never have to endure this. If she had known this was his plan, she would have stopped the damned man long before he ever thought about bringing himself here.

Eldridge's breath stirred her hair. "He lost his sister. She wandered off into the snow and no one knew what had happened to her, or how to find her. It took them seven weeks to find the little sprite again."

"And then? Was the little girl alive?" She stiffened, hoping that the child hadn't been found frozen to the ground.

"She was fine." He chuckled in her ear. "She'd just wanted some adventure and a change of pace. So she'd gone into the forest where the trees talked and the wind whispered secrets in her ears. She was a faerie child, after all, and everything out there called to her."

Freya lifted her head from his shoulder to glare at him. "Did you steal my sister because you thought you could replicate this story?"

He shrugged. "Maybe a little. Your sister did want to come to the faerie realm, though. She practically begged us to kidnap her in the hopes you wouldn't come thundering after her like some great beast assured that we were damaging her honor."

"Well, you did." Freya thought back to her sister's fluffy white tail and sighed. "No one would ever marry her in the mortal realm now. She couldn't even become a spinster with me, heaven's forbid. That tail would have people putting her on a bonfire faster than they could say witch."

Eldridge tugged her back into the haven of his arms and his laughter rumbled through his chest. "I think she would be honored to be called a witch. Esther seems more interested in that lifestyle than you."

"You're right, she probably would have practiced magic if I had let her."

Freya could just see it now. Her sister would have taken strengthening the wards into creating her own. Then she would have tried to spell a few things in their house to move on their own, and suddenly they would have been two witches living in a hut together. The villagers would have hated it, but Esther might have actually been happy.

Ridiculous, but her sister had always been the adventurous one.

Underneath her fingers, the open wounds moved. The skin shifted and shuddered as though there were snakes underneath her hands. Freya gasped and then realized the skin was knitting back together. All his wounds were closing, progressing with each inhalation that the Goblin King drew.

He was healing himself.

How?

Those wounds had nearly been fatal. She had seen them herself, had felt the blood on her fingers.

Drawing away from his embrace, she lifted her hands and stared down at the blood that still coated them. The liquid was still sticky and warm. But the wounds she had been touching were no longer there.

"How?" she whispered.

Freya moved forward and caught the edge of his ragged shirt in her hands. She lifted it up and over his head, revealing lean planes of muscles and ribs that were too harsh. But not a single wound remained open on his blood slicked chest.

She pressed her fingers to where she had known there was a weeping hole. "How is this possible?" she whispered.

"Anything is possible here, remember?"

The expression on his face tugged at her heartstrings. He looked at her as though she were made of magic. Maybe she was. After all, it was her life force that had healed him.

She released a ragged groan, then threw herself into his arms. Freya kissed him as she'd desired for so long. Open mouthed, rough, and raw. She poured all her worries and fears into the kiss.

Gnashing teeth bit at lips and she didn't care if it hurt him. He could handle a little more pain as punishment for all that he'd put her through.

"How dare you put yourself in danger like that," she hissed against his tongue. "You chose to do this to yourself."

"I did, but never again." He vowed. His fingers flexed against her sides, dragging her closer.

As if she could get any closer to him. Freya was pressed to his body from thighs to shoulders. She wanted to crawl inside him, or perhaps for him to crawl inside her. It didn't matter. She needed to be tighter against him. To get to a point where she didn't feel like they were two people, but one.

She clawed at his chest with her hands. Her palms couldn't get enough of the heat that now poured off him in waves. The muscles bunched underneath her fingers, beckoning her to touch more. To drag at his flesh and press her lips where her fingers had just claimed.

Freya had never felt like this. She'd never been so consumed by desire that she didn't know which way was up or down. It didn't matter. Direction, sense, self, all of it fell in the wake of her passion.

Eldridge flexed his hands at her waist again and then gripped with a punishing strength. He lifted her up, scooping his arms underneath her thighs and forcing her to wrap her legs around his waist. She balanced herself on his shoulders, drinking in his kisses like fine wine.

She knew wherever he touched would be bruised, or perhaps he'd only leave red marks. But the thought gave her a thrill that rocked through her entire body. She was slick and overheated, needing him to touch everything and nothing at once.

If he touched more, she feared she'd lose herself to his passion. But if he didn't touch more of her, then Freya was certain she would die. Either was a horrific and entirely unsatisfying end to something so thoroughly wonderful.

Eldridge groaned into her lips and pulled himself free from her kisses. She let out a tiny sound of disapproval before silencing herself. He had only moved away to put his lips to her neck.

Dragging his teeth and tongue down the long column, he hissed out a breath. "You hold yourself with such swan-like grace. You will surely be my undoing, you beautiful woman."

She shouldn't have been so proud that she had distracted him, and yet, the words sent a zing of passion straight into her belly. "Good," she replied. "I want to be your undoing, Goblin King. I want to unmake you so that you are something new. Something whole. And mine."

He drew back then, releasing his hold on her neck to stare deeply into her eyes. "Haven't you already seen? You have made me into a new man already, Freya. I hardly recognize myself in the mirror, but I think I like this version better than what I was before."

All the stars in the skies reflected in his eyes. She could see a thousand galaxies, a thousand possibilities all waiting for her there.

She opened her mouth, likely to let her emotions spill from her tongue.

Someone cleared their throat in the doorway. The sound of Arrow's padding footsteps entered the room, and everything came crashing down around her ears.

The Goblin Queen.

The throne.

A life that she would have to take.

And they were kissing in private, like they were two teenagers trying to sneak away from their parents.

Cheeks burning red hot, she untangled her legs from around the Goblin King's waist and cleared her throat. "Arrow. It's good to see you. I apologize."

The Goblin King also cleared his throat, the tops of his silver cheeks darker than the rest. "Give me a moment, would you? I need to put myself back together, apparently. This is…"

He didn't finish the sentence. The Goblin King walked straight through the wall and disappeared.

CHAPTER 23

Freya crossed her arms over her chest and decided not to look at the smug expression on Arrow's face. And she knew it would be there. She didn't even have to look at the dog to know that he was grinning from ear to ear.

"Stop," she muttered.

"Stop what?"

"Stop looking at me like that." She had never hit a dog in her life, but Freya thought it entirely likely that she could if he didn't turn around and leave the room.

"I'm not doing anything. You were the one just kissing the Goblin King like he was hiding something behind his tongue. Did you find anything, by the way? I know a lot of ladies are very curious whether or not he's got a secret back there or if he's just a boring kisser."

Actually, Arrow wasn't even a dog. He was a goblin who looked like a dog, and she thought that meant it was fine for her to kick him. Maybe a few times before she threw him out of the room and then buried her head in the snow.

How was she supposed to look at the Goblin King again after that? He had completely crawled his way underneath her skin and more. He looked at her like... like...

Well, as though he enjoyed her company. As though he enjoyed kissing her, and that was a problem. They couldn't kiss each other when there was a Goblin Queen to kill, a throne to save, and her sister back in the Autumn Court who was apparently falling head over heels for a goblin too.

No. Freya stopped that thought process. She was not falling in love with a goblin, just like her sister. She couldn't. Goblins and humans didn't mix, and she was leaving it at that.

"Arrow," she snarled. "You will keep this to yourself. Do you hear me?"

He pressed a paw to his muzzle, miming that he was going to keep his mouth shut. But somehow, she doubted that he was going to do that at all. There was too much mischief in his eyes, mixed with a very healthy dose of pleasure that he had finally caught them.

Where was Eldridge anyway?

He said he had to go put himself together, which she could only hope meant he was as affected by their kiss as she had been. Or was that even a kiss at this point?

She wandered over to the ice block of a bed and sat down on the edge. Pressing her fingertips to her lips, she stared at the empty fireplace and tried very hard to not think about what had just happened. She needed to force her thoughts back to what they were about to do.

She needed to think about anything other than his taste that still lingered on her tongue. Or the way he had gripped her hips like she was his only lifeline. Or the sounds he made in her ear when he had shifted away from her mouth and down her neck...

Arrow cleared his throat again. He sat directly in front of her, though she didn't know when he had gotten there. How had he moved without her realizing it?

"What?" she asked.

He looked pointedly at her neck and then back to her gaze. "I think you'll want to cover that up before we see the Goblin Queen."

"Cover what up?"

"The giant red mark that Eldridge left." His tongue lolled out of the side of his mouth and his eyes danced with laughter. "I think trying to convince the Queen that you mean her no harm will be a little difficult when you let the love of the Queen's life put a hickey on your neck."

"He did not!" Freya lunged back to her feet, trying to find a piece of ice that was at least a little reflective. "Did he?"

Of course, there wasn't any reflective ice in the damn room. She needed to know now if the Goblin King had marked her.

Arrow trotted to the bed and hopped up onto the icy block. "I thought the King would be a lot worse for wear than what it appeared he was. How strange. I guess I overestimated the Queen's hatred. She didn't really hurt him all that much. And here I was assuming we'd get him back in pieces."

Freya stopped her frustrated searching and shook her head. "No, she did hurt him. He was stuck to crystals in the floor like they were daggers. I helped to heal him."

"You did?" Arrow's jaw dropped open. He sank back onto his haunches and then lifted a paw to tap his muzzle in thought. "How is it possible that a mortal healed a faerie? And a king at that?"

"He took some of my magic," she replied. "Or something like that. I'm not sure. Remember when I said he could take some of my life force if he needed to? Well, he did. Again."

That damned jaw remained open. Arrow stared at her as though she'd grown a third head.

She frowned, looked around her, and then asked, "What?"

"You healed him?"

"Apparently. I think it's more accurate to say he healed himself and used what little magic he could take from me." But he was still looking at her strangely, and she could only assume that meant something was very, very wrong. "Arrow, why are you making that face?"

"Well... I..." His tail thumped once, twice on the bed behind him. "Humans can't do that."

"I don't think you're right, because I most certainly did. He took whatever he wanted. I could feel him doing it. Just the faintest tug, like he was pulling something out of me." She shuddered. "I don't want to feel that again."

"Miss Freya, what I'm trying to say is... Well. Mortals don't have magic. If you were entirely human yourself, then you wouldn't have been able to give him any magic at all. Pulling a life force to make his projection easier to see, that's one thing. But healing him physically?" He looked her up and down, almost suspiciously. "I suppose that tells us why you were able to hold your own against the Goblin King all this time."

Her mind refused to believe what he was saying.

She was just a human. Both she and her sister were mortal. They came from the realm where magic was a struggle and only performed by those with questionable morals. That was the truth, plain and simple.

"That's not possible," she said. "I know my history. I know my family. There is no magic in my line, Arrow. I'm just mortal."

He grinned. "I guess you were wrong."

Freya didn't want to argue with him, but she could prove that there was no magic in her blood whatsoever. Opening her mouth to begin, she was stopped by a door on the interior of her room slamming open. She hadn't even known there was another door in this room.

Flinching, she leapt away from the fireplace and back into a safe corner of the room. The Goblin King strode through the new doorway, straightening the fine lines of his crushed velvet suit that he so dearly loved.

And that she very much appreciated him wearing.

Though he was still too thin, and that would take time to fix, the suit hugged his muscles in a very satisfying and distracting way. His shoulders bunched as he reached up and tugged the wrist of his shirt into place. "This is so much better, don't you think?"

Arrow practically wiggled in his place on the bed. He stood up onto his back legs and bowed deeply. "My King. You look the same as the first day I met you. Impressive. Delightfully powerful. I am surprised you managed after all the Queen had intended to do."

He looked at the goblin dog and grinned, sharp teeth glinting in the dim light. "Arrow. My old friend, I should have known you would be the one to guide the hero of this story. And I thought you wouldn't step foot in the Winter Court ever again."

"Only once in a blue moon," Arrow replied.

"And it will be a blue moon when we are done, my friend. Mark my words, we are going to change the very fabric of time." His eyes flashed bright and filled with malice. "Lumi won't know what hit her, poor dear. But I should have done this a long time ago."

Freya was still stuck on their previous conversation. She wasn't mortal? That couldn't be possible. Her mother wouldn't have hated faeries as she had throughout their life. One couldn't hate a person for being faerie, but then love her daughters who were of the same blood. Such complicated emotions weren't... well. She supposed they were entirely possible after all.

Had her mother experienced something tragic? Was her father not even her real blood sire? After all, Freya had always thought she looked more like her father than her mother, because the similarities were obviously there.

And her mother wasn't a faerie. She was certain of that. Her father couldn't have been. He was too simple of a man and had never been interested in magic like her mother. He was more interested in farming than wards or spells.

Freya's mother was obsessed with the faerie realm. She was obsessed with magic and all the things that came with it. But only to prevent anything from happening to her family.

Right?

Wasn't that the way of it?

"Freya," the Goblin King's voice broke through her thoughts. "Are you ready?"

Ready for what? Freya wasn't ready for anything. She wanted to reach through the veil of death and strangle her mother for leaving nothing but questions in her wake. It wasn't fair that Freya was left here with Esther and no one else to answer the questions of their lineage.

"Hmm?" she settled on asking. She looked up into his frowning face and wondered what he saw behind her eyes.

"We have to focus." His tone was almost scolding, and he had every right to do so.

Freya knew what they had to do would be very difficult. They both needed to focus on everything that was about to come to pass. They had to be ready for whatever the Goblin Queen might throw at them.

And instead, she was standing here with her head in the clouds, completely incapable of listening to anything. "I'm sorry. I was caught up in my own thoughts for a bit. What were you saying?"

"I was telling you my plan," he replied, frowning. "Did you hear any of it?"

"No." Freya at least could answer honestly, considering this was a very important plan that she needed to be ready for. "Tell me again, Eldridge. I have a lot on my mind."

His expression softened, and he reached to touch a finger to her chin. "Yes, you do. You play a very important part in this, my dear, and I'm sorry for it. We're going to her banquet, together. She likely has no idea I've escaped her prison, or there would be a thousand of her self made guards running around this palace. We'll catch her by surprise and force her to see us as actual threats."

It was as good a plan as they were going to get. She realized just how much of a stretch this was. The Goblin Queen might be surprised for a few moments, but that was all they had. The woman thought on her feet with the best of warriors, ready to plan her battle at a moment's notice.

"Understood," she replied. "And while we're at the banquet, how am I supposed to get close enough to kill her?"

"While we dance, of course. Lumi was always the one who wanted to see everything go as planned. She loves anything that requires her to be the most beautiful woman in the room. I will force her to wake up more of the Winter Court. Bring them all to the dance floor, and then we will show her what true beauty is. We'll frustrate her. Anger her. Put her in a position where she feels like she has to prove herself." Eldridge reached for her waist, tucking her against his side once more. "She will hate you. And that is when we will strike."

Right, like that was going to work. Freya wasn't more beautiful than the Winter Princess who was now the Goblin Queen. A woman with that much magic at her fingertips would make a mortal look plain and boring.

She pointed to the white dress crumpled in the back of the room. The fur coat sat next to it, now slightly yellowed with age. "That's all I have to wear, unless you want me to show her up in a plain brown traveling gown."

Freya wiggled out of his arms and lifted her hands over her head. She gave him a little spin, showing just how plain she was.

His plan required a beauty. A woman who could outshine even the brightest of stars. And what he had was a vaguely polished rock, but still a stone from a riverbed.

Eldridge smiled, and the expression lit up the room. His hands glowed with power and he lifted them to gesture up and down her body. "You are more lovely than you know, Freya. But you will not walk into her ballroom as one of the Winter Court as she would so like to claim you. You are mine, and thus you will be dressed in the regalia of my true court."

She felt the magic before he even started. It tickled her feet, tingling around her legs and sweeping up her frame. The fabric of her dress unlaced itself, changing structure and form, weaving into something new and entirely different.

Dark amethyst spread from the bottom of her new gown. Tiny sparkles of silver stars dusted the hem near her feet, then cinched her waist in tight with more tiny stars. Moons and planets spread up the bodice that hugged her small waist and drew her chest up higher. A thin cloak of midnight blue clasped around her neck, decorated with diamonds that sparkled as she moved. Freya felt her hair slithering up the back of her neck, becoming an intricate coil of braids and loose tendrils of curls.

Suddenly, she was no longer the same woman. She was beautiful and remarkable, a faerie princess rather than a human who happened to find herself in this miraculous place.

Freya smoothed a hand down her bodice, the boning nearly uncomfortably tight, then looked back up to Eldridge's pleased expression. "Well, do I look like a woman who could distract the Goblin Queen?"

He held out his hand for her to take. "Yes, Freya. But you were always that woman, regardless of the clothing. Did you not see the jealousy in the Goblin Queen's eyes when you were changing? She wanted to make you ugly. She did not succeed."

His words seemed like a stretch, but she would take the compliment. Freya slipped her arm through his. "Are you ready to kill a queen, my king?"

He grinned. "Oh, I've been ready for a very long time."

CHAPTER 24

They walked through the halls of the palace toward the
room where this had all started. Or at least, the first
time Freya had actually talked with the Queen rather
than shivered with fear. The hall where ballerinas had danced
until their feet bled. The place where frozen food had proven
this quest to be more difficult than she had thought it would be.

Teeth chattering, Freya looked up at Eldridge who was
quickly looking to be more himself. His cheeks were rounding
back to their normal chiseled form. And when he turned his
head to meet her gaze, he didn't appear nervous at all. Instead,
his eyes were lit with excitement.

"Everything is going to work out as planned," he said. "You
shouldn't be so worried, Freya."

She wasn't a fool. Things could easily fall by the wayside if
they underestimated the Queen. After all, hadn't he made the
same mistake with Freya herself?

"I think we should prepare for anything," she replied. "What
is the plan if this doesn't work?"

"It will work."

"And if it doesn't?" she insisted.

He paused them in front of the banquet hall door, his hand

braced on the icy surface. "We're going to keep her off guard. That's the plan. If it fails, then we fail. So we will keep ourselves ready for anything and everything that she might throw at us. Because she will throw everything she knows. Thankfully, I happen to understand her thoughts. I grew up with her. I know what she's going to do."

And Freya had grown up with Esther. She'd never guessed her sister would take something from goblins, let alone be happy to live among them.

"Trust me," he reiterated.

She would try her best. But Freya feared he was making a grave mistake. One they couldn't so easily come back from.

Eldridge closed his eyes, and she saw his hands start to glow. The warmth of his magic spread through the door, melting the icy structures and turning it back into warm mahogany wood.

Freya gasped in surprise as the magic spread. Ice fell in great, slushy waves that soaked the cold floor, warming the ground and heating it back to the original white marble. His magic spread even further, pulsing down the hall and no doubt into the room where the Goblin Queen waited for them.

Only once the hallway was unrecognizable did he stop. And though he was still weak, he held himself with pride in the set of his shoulders, then smiled at Freya. "Now we're ready."

He shoved the doors open and held out his arm for her to take. Freya slipped her hand onto his forearm and allowed him to guide her into a completely different ballroom.

The walls were painted bright yellow with tiny daisies falling from the ceiling that was made of stained glass. Silver metal ivy crawled over each individual panel. All the seats had melted from their icy structures, back into the warm, caramel wood. The Queen waited at a banquet table where there was a mountain of food and steaming liquids.

Freya's gaze flicked to the back wall where the dancers had emerged from the frozen waterfall. Now, it was a bubbling fountain, impressively large, with brightly colored goldfish swimming within it.

The Goblin Queen's chair screeched as she shoved it back. "What is the manner of this magic?"

She wore a pale blue gown made of ice. The bodice stretched up toward her neck in tendrils frozen to her skin. The fabric hugged her beautiful form, and her white hair was piled atop her head with long pillars of white ice as a crown. She was as lovely as ever, and suddenly, Freya felt plain again.

Eldridge swept into a low bow, tugging Freya with him. "I thought the castle should return to its former glory. All this frozen nonsense would make the Queen ill. You know how she hated the cold."

The words were a challenge. The Goblin Queen braced her hands on the table in front of her and snarled, "You're looking at the Queen, Eldridge. And you know I always loved the cold. No matter how much my dearly departed mother wanted to wipe it from existence."

"You would have been happier if you listened to her tastes. She was always more interesting than you, however. She was ready to take the world by storm. And you?" He tilted his head to the side, looking her over as if he was disappointed. "You turned into the spitting image of the woman your parents never wanted you to be."

"Such a shame." The Goblin Queen rounded the table, her hands glowing bright blue at her sides. "And yet, I'm more myself than I've ever been. Perhaps they were flawed parents who never saw the use in a daughter so powerful. How did you get out of your prison, Eldridge? I hope you enjoyed your adventure, because I'm afraid you need to go back now."

"I won't be doing that." He tugged Freya closer to his side. "You suspected nothing when we were right under your nose. I'm disappointed, Lumi. I thought you would be better at sniffing out a rat."

Freya bristled at the term. They were talking like she wasn't even there, and this wasn't the plan. Wasn't she supposed to be the one distracting the Queen?

But this conversation felt personal. These were two siblings who were fighting about everything they could. Each word was a barb meant to wriggle under the other's skin, and for what?

They would not change each other's minds. And throwing insults like this would not make anyone feel better.

The Goblin Queen tilted her head back and laughed. "Eldridge! This adorable rebellion is cute, it really is. But nothing is going to stop me. Not you. Not your little human pet. Did you think I didn't know you were talking to her?"

"You didn't," Freya interjected. "You let me wander about the castle unsupervised."

"He wasn't in the castle, darling. The longer you spent searching these halls, the more time I could take his magic. And now he has none at all." The Goblin Queen's smile was sharp and cold. "That was the last of it, wasn't it? One more trick. A show that would make me think you still had power. I know you, Eldridge. And I know when you are weak."

He stiffened. "Perhaps," Eldridge replied. "But you don't know everything, Lumi."

The blue light of her magic spread from her fingertips. It touched the table first, turning all the food back into frozen chunks of ice. The tendrils of cold spread across the floor, reaching the fountain where it shifted the water back into its original rigid structure.

Eldridge did nothing to stop the magic from spreading. Maybe the Goblin Queen was right. He had used the last bit of magic that he'd stolen from Freya to turn this room into something warm and more inviting.

He watched the magic spread with a bored expression. "Lumi. Are we going to fight by turning the room from cold to warm? I came here to offer a truce. Why don't we dance like we did in the old days? Wake the court up. Bring at least a few of them back so we can enjoy each other's company. I'm bored staying in the prison cell."

The magic paused at his offer. "Is that why you're here?" The Goblin Queen asked with a laugh. "Eldridge. You know I'm not going to let you out. And I'm not going to have a dance."

"I think you will," he replied. "For old time's sake."

The Queen drew in a deep breath. She looked Eldridge up and down as though thoroughly disappointed. "Is this your plan? To make me wake up the court and then convince them to rebel against me? You're too weak, Eldridge. And you forgot that I am no fool."

"But you are a fool who loves me," he replied. He released his hold on Freya and took a step closer to the Goblin Queen. "I'm asking for one little thing. A favor, if you will."

"You think this will distract me," the Goblin Queen said. She shook her head in disbelief. "You think a dance will be the end of this all. What is your plan? To try to kill me once we all spin wildly across the floor?"

"Wouldn't it be a fitting end to our story?"

"There is no fitting end to our story. You want me to die so you can take the throne back. I'm not going to give you that satisfaction." She leaned around him, staring at Freya with death in her eyes. "Once I put you back in your prison, I'm going to take your pet apart piece by piece. We'll see just how brave she can be. I've always wondered what was inside a mortal, you see. We don't get them around here so often."

Eldridge lunged forward and caught Lumi's face in both hands. He forced her to look at him, his hands shaking with some unnamed emotion. "Lumi," he whispered. The word was guttural with emotion. "I'm begging you."

Freya's heart fell into the pit of her stomach. She'd heard those tones before, but they were always when he was trying to seduce her. Watching him do that to another woman was like breaking apart pieces of her soul and tossing them into a river. The Goblin Queen didn't have to rip her apart, after all.

She hurt. Physically, even though she hadn't realized that was possible. Her entire body ached as though she'd been in a fight, or a battle, or perhaps only realized that a Goblin King had many layers to him and some of them were at her own expense.

Lumi melted at his touch. She moved closer to the king as though her body couldn't stay away from him. "You want a ball so desperately, but my dearest, my love. You won't defeat me while we're dancing. I will make you regret ever trying to beat me."

"That's a bet I'm willing to take," he replied. Eldridge released her and stepped away, tucking his hands behind his back and clearing his throat. "If you think you can prevent us from stopping you, then please. By all means. Lumi, I want to see if you can do it."

"A test then?" The Goblin Queen tucked her own hands behind her back and turned. She sat down at the banquet table and touched a finger to her chin. "You believe you can stop me. I believe you can't. Whoever remains alive by the end of the ball will win. How does that sound?"

Awful. Freya wanted to step in and tell them both that they were being foolish. No one could win a bet like that. No one could possibly make that bet thinking that either of them would triumph. They would just lock horns for the entire ball and then... what?

Eldridge nodded. "Of course, that sounds like a deal to me. And if no one wins by the end? If we're both alive?"

Exactly, that's what Freya would have asked. Obviously they needed to come to some kind of understanding. The likely end was that neither of them would kill the other.

The Goblin Queen tapped a long-nailed finger against her chin. "Then I win. You return to your cell like a good little goblin, and I get to do whatever I want with your human pet."

Absolutely not. They could not agree to a deal with her like that, because then they would always lose no matter what. Freya knew for a fact she wouldn't be able to put a dagger through this woman's heart in that amount of time. It was just impossible.

The Goblin King wouldn't be so foolish. Eldridge was a risk taker, yes, and he enjoyed a battle of wits. But a ball wasn't enough time to get everything aligned that needed to be aligned.

Freya looked to him for a scoff, or an angry snort that the Queen would try to pull the wool over their eyes like that.

But her heart stilled when she saw his expression. That calculating look was him considering it. And worse?

He nodded.

The Goblin King agreed to the deal. "We'll accept your deal. If we don't kill you by the end of this, then you win."

"And what do I win?" The Goblin Queen asked. She leaned forward, nearly crawling onto the table as she awaited his answer. "I want to hear you say the words, Eldridge. I want to know that this deal is exactly what you have always feared."

He cleared his throat and avoided Freya's questioning gaze. She would have stepped in front of him if it wouldn't have ruined their plan.

But she had to try something. "No," Freya interrupted them. "This is a losing deal. We won't take this one, nor any other with the likes of you."

The Goblin Queen looked at her with a bored glance. "Dear, he's already accepted. We can't go back on that now. What we have to decide is what the other person wins."

Well, that couldn't be Eldridge. He wasn't going back to the prison, or she'd failed in everything she'd attempted. Freya created a shield of her own body, shoved in front of Eldridge, and squared her shoulders. "Then you win me."

The Queen laughed so hard the sound turned into unladylike snorts. "Do you think I want you more than him? That's adorable. Really, Eldridge, I understand your interest in the little thing now. She is a cute little adventurer, isn't she?"

Freya bristled at the tone. She was more than just adorable or cute. She was the mortal who had defeated the Goblin King, and she could do it with this witch as well.

Eldridge put his hand on her shoulder and moved her back beside him. "No, Freya. You aren't going to offer yourself up for this deal. Obviously the Goblin Queen only has one desire, and I'm more than happy to put it on the line." He straightened his shoulders, inclined his head, and replied, "You will win me, Lumi. We all know that's what you want."

Every fiber of Freya's being screamed with rage. Why would he do that? Why would he offer the one thing they couldn't give?

Grinding her teeth, Freya clutched the fabric of her skirts in her fists and tried to stay quiet. She'd yell at him later, if she got the chance. But he had to stop making these decisions without her.

Otherwise, they'd keep getting into situations like this.

Lumi grinned, then lifted her hands and clapped them loudly. "So be it, Eldridge. You have yourself a deal. Now, the Winter Court is waking and we shall throw a ball unlike any this court has ever seen before."

CHAPTER 25

Freya flinched away from the doors as they slammed open again. She feared they had both been unaware as the Goblin Queen's icy creatures snuck up behind them. The Goblin Queen didn't care about honor, she could easily have been distracting them while her magic built giant beings to throw them both into prison.

But it wasn't an army that entered the banquet hall.

Faeries flooded into the room. They were the same faeries she remembered from when she had first come to this terrifying court. Each one was beautiful with delicate butterfly-like wings. Some large. Some small. Frost patterns decorated their cheeks and any skin that was bare from their clothing.

Their dresses were made of gossamer. Their suits of fine linen and silk. Pale blues. Beautiful, deep midnights. Every color was a shade of blue and so incredibly appealing. Snowflakes and ice made a prominent feature in all the clothing that the faeries wore.

But they all had a similar expression of confusion on their face. None of them seemed to understand where they were, or how they had come to the ballroom.

The Goblin Queen stood, clapped her hands for attention,

then smiled at the members of her court. "Welcome home," she said. "You've all been asleep for quite some time. But you're back now. So you might as well make a show of it. The previous Goblin King has asked for a ball. We will remember him fondly now that he passes the crown to me. The rightful goblin heir."

The winter couple nearest to Freya bristled. They looked at each other with horror in their eyes, before turning back to stare at the Goblin Queen. They wisely kept their mouths shut, but Freya knew what they were thinking.

What had happened while they slept?

Why had all their nightmares become reality?

Music danced through the air. At some point, a few faeries of the Winter Court had walked to the back hall and brought out instruments. Violins, cellos, even harps were dragged from some hidden room and set up away from the others. All strings, Freya noted. The musicians lifted their instruments, saluted the Queen, then filled the air with the haunting tones of the Winter Court.

Snowflakes fell from the ceiling. And though it was strange, they never touched the ground. Freya reached up and caught one on her fingertip.

It was as lovely as it was delicate. The snowflake hovered for a second on her finger before melting into a small teardrop. She couldn't help but fear the tiny thing was a metaphor for Freya herself. A mortal in a faerie court. Caught between two nobles who wanted to destroy each other.

How was she supposed to survive this?

The Winter Court drifted into their places as though the entire dance was choreographed. They raised their arms as one, took their dance partners into their embraces, and then whirled into an intricate dance. They moved so quickly that Freya had a hard time guessing what the steps even were.

This was different than the ballerinas who had twirled like tops spinning out of control. Every couple was perfect. Their steps were measured, and they weren't just dancing because the

Goblin Queen bid them to. They were dancing in happiness at finally being awake.

They had each other again. Their arms full of someone they loved. Even if their new Queen was a monster.

The winter faeries wrapped each other up with warmth and affection. They whispered endearments in each other's ears and how much they had missed each other. That dreams couldn't hold a candle to the reality of holding a loved one in their arms.

The Goblin King stepped up to her, reached out his arms, and waited until Freya looked at him. He fit in here among these faeries. She hadn't realized how much until she saw them all together.

The Autumn Court was one thing. Those creatures with mixed animal features had wiggled their way into her heart. They were the misfits, the unfortunate, and the odd. But that wasn't who the Goblin King was.

Each faerie in the Winter Court was a masterpiece of perfection. And so was the Goblin King. His cold features, the silver skin, even the tufts of hair on his ears were meant for this place.

Perfection could not stand flaws. Freya had many.

"I don't think I can do this," she whispered. She stared at him with fear shaking every limb. "I think we're going to lose, Eldridge. And I don't want all of this to be for nothing."

"We aren't going to lose." He winked. "Didn't I tell you to trust me?"

"I do trust you." Or at least, she should. But this moment felt like he had no control, and neither did she.

Eldridge lifted a brow, impatience radiating in his expression and the set of his shoulders. So, she allowed him to pull her into his arms and thrust her into the dance.

She couldn't say she doubted him. Of course she trusted the Goblin King. Eldridge was a mastermind at using other people's emotions to get them to do what he wanted. He'd played her easier than the musicians were playing their instruments. He knew every thought in Freya's head, and he certainly knew how to play the Goblin Queen, too.

But she didn't think this was the right way to go about it. She didn't think they would win this wild game. And she believed they would regret these decisions. Every single horrible choice would put them right back to square one.

Eldridge tugged her closer, pressing her against his pounding heart. "You are worried," he murmured in her ear. "I can still feel it. So can the Goblin Queen. You need to control yourself and know that I would never let anything happen to you."

"I'm not worried about myself," she corrected. His hands flexed at her waist, then he lifted her up as all the other faeries did with their partners.

Freya watched the fabric of their gowns spin. For a moment, she could pretend they weren't even in the Winter Court. All this magical movement was like a dream. Like she had been transported into a fairytale story that her mother would tell her as a child. Of gowns and princesses falling in love with princes at a ball.

When her feet hit the ground again, she wrapped her arms around Eldridge's neck and inhaled his familiar scent. "I'm worried about you."

"There's no need. We're going to win." His eyes strayed toward the Goblin Queen where she was surveying the dancers. Likely to pick out who her partner would be. "The Goblin Queen's faults are the same as mine were. She thinks too highly of herself and that will be her downfall."

"Isn't it dangerous to assume it won't be yours? You still have that flaw, Eldridge."

He shook his head in clear denial. "She will do everything that I want her to do. I would fall for this trap, and so shall she."

And there it was. He already illustrated that he understood why she was so nervous. He said the words she had feared he would say, but he didn't understand that he was falling right into the same web he thought he'd spun for her.

"Eldridge, listen to me."

But he was already lost. The Goblin Queen beckoned him to her side, and he went like a moth to the flame. The partners in the dance changed. She was thrust into the arms of a man with blue hair and eyes black as coal.

He leaned closer to her and whispered, "You've already lost him. Why don't you entertain yourself with me for a little while?"

She smiled at the man when he leaned away. This was a game she knew how to play. A faerie tried to distract her, and Freya was getting rather good at telling them off.

This man was just as impressive as the others. His suit was finely pressed, with miniscule white snowflakes on his shoulders that grew larger until they met the hem at the bottom of his jacket. His blue hair was perfectly quaffed. Handsome, yes, but those black eyes lacked the emotion of the other faeries.

She didn't trust him. Freya kept the false smile on her lips and replied, "While I'm certain you would be a wonderful choice, I'm afraid I can't give up on him just yet."

The faerie looked surprised that she would deny him. "Why would you care what a fallen king does? He's already walking to his own ruin, little human. At least you'd be safe with me."

"Would I?" She didn't think she would be safe with anyone.

Eldridge swung the Goblin Queen into a wild dance. He spun her closer and closer to Freya, and she knew this was the moment. She was supposed to reach into her pocket and pull out the knife. Then, when he got close enough, she would simply hold it out. Together, they would slice through the Goblin Queen and spill her blood on the floor like rubies.

But the faerie who was holding onto her suddenly tightened his grip. He clutched her against his chest, the grip punishing. Bruising. The bones of her arms creaked in the tight squeeze. She lost all the breath in her lungs.

Eyes wide, she met that black gaze with realization dawning.

He grinned down at her with sharp, shark-like teeth. "None

of this is real, Freya. Did you think she would risk losing control for even a second?"

"Eldridge," she croaked. "It's a trap."

And of course it would be. The Goblin Queen was no fool.

All she saw before everything exploded was the wide-eyed stare Eldridge gave her. He looked like he was shocked that the Queen had beaten him. But that always had been his downfall, hadn't it?

He underestimated the people who wanted to overthrow him. He underestimated Freya and now he underestimated the Winter Princess who was far more capable than Freya could ever be.

Time slowed, then stopped. All the faeries froze in place once again. Solid structures wearing expressions of horror. Their time in the living world had been short, but now they were thrust back into the dreaming realm where they would likely remain for the rest of their lives.

The Goblin Queen didn't freeze Freya. But that was expected. She wanted the mortal to see what happened when someone tried to beat a Goblin Queen.

Eldridge coughed. The ragged, rough sound preceded a bright blossom of blood that stained his berry red lips. The floor warped and ice surrounded his feet. Holding him in place.

He swung a clawed hand that froze solid just before the Queen's neck. He would have killed her if the wicked tips of his fingers had touched her throat. But of course, they didn't. Nothing sharp would ever touch a woman that powerful. Not unless she wanted it to.

His beloved face turned bright blue, just like all the other frozen faeries. The ice consumed him until the Goblin King wasn't even a prisoner anymore.

He was a decoration piece.

Freya's breath fogged in the air. The room turned even more frigid as the Goblin Queen stared at the man she had finally ruined. After all this time, perhaps centuries planning her revenge, she had turned the Goblin King into nothing more than her own personal plaything.

"Don't you think he looks better this way?" The Goblin Queen asked. "I think he looks more like someone we could both handle. Don't you, my dear?"

Freya didn't know how to respond. The tears in her eyes blurred her surroundings. She could make out the strange, frozen shapes of the faeries who had returned to their previous forms. But it seemed like there were more shadows walking among them. Shadows that looked like the spirits of those who had lost their lives once again.

She swallowed hard, biting the insides of her cheeks so the tears didn't fall. "I prefer him warm and moving."

"Of course you do." The Goblin Queen rolled her eyes and turned back to Freya. "You would have wanted him to beat me. You wanted to help this story become something others would talk about for ages, didn't you? All at my expense."

"Yes." What reason did she have to lie? Freya told the truth. She was trapped. The frozen faerie's arms were still wrapped tightly around her, and there was nothing she could do to get out of them. She wasn't strong enough to break the man's arms. And she wouldn't want to, even if she could.

The Goblin Queen meandered to her side, hands pressed against the bodice of her icy gown. "So what was the plan, Freya?"

"We were going to kill you," she replied. "The ball was supposed to be a ruse so that you would let your guard down. Then we would have an opening to remove you from the throne."

"I'm sure that was a good plan at the time. But you had forgotten the most dangerous thing that Eldridge taught me." She leaned in close and pressed her icy lips against Freya's ear. "I trust no one."

And if Eldridge had listened to Freya, then they wouldn't have been in this mess. They might have succeeded. But no. Of course not. They were in his old home and he was the one who knew best.

She wished she could go back in time and slap some sense into the idiot. At least then she wouldn't have to face down this terrifying woman all on her own. And the reality was that there were no more moves in this chess game.

No one could stop the Goblin Queen, now.

Arrow was safely in their room, waiting for Eldridge and Freya to return. He wouldn't come looking for them for a while. Plenty of time for the Goblin Queen to rip Freya into pieces. Just as she had told Eldridge that she would.

Freya was well and truly alone.

Biting her lip, she decided to take control over her own fate. "What do you want?"

The Goblin Queen blinked her long, white lashes. "Excuse me?"

"You wouldn't keep me alive unless you wanted something from me. You're talking, asking me to tell you our plan, for what reason? You're stalling. Or you want something from me and you're trying to figure out the best way to ask it. So go ahead." She hoped she was right. Freya was making the biggest mistake of her life if she wasn't. "What do you want from me, Goblin Queen?"

And there it was. The light that burned in Lumi's eyes when she thought she had trapped someone. The Goblin Queen drew herself up straighter. Her hands left her waist and floated at her sides as though she were preparing to cast some spell. But she didn't.

Instead, the Goblin Queen grinned that pointy smile and said, "You can still save him, Freya. And I want to know if you're willing to give up everything to see the Goblin King breathe again."

Freya's eyes widened. "Save him? You're the one who cast the spell to freeze him. You're the only one who can save him now, not me."

"Oh, you see, this is all his doing. The Winter Court is still under the curse he laid on us all those years ago. We are frozen, and though I can lift the curse for some time, it's difficult to battle for more than just myself." The Goblin Queen sighed, then pressed her hands to her heart. "It takes a toll on me. Or had you forgotten how easily you discovered I'm using three sources of magic to keep myself awake?"

Was that the truth of it, then? Had they missed something so simple, so easy to discover, and yet there it was?

Eldridge's magic was powerful. He had complete control over all the magic given to the Goblin heir, but also the magic that was innately his. So of course the curse he had cast upon this place would be more powerful than the average spell.

The Goblin Queen was trying to stay awake.

Freya let out a low breath of shock. "Of course," she muttered. "That's why you're always using magic. You're still fighting against his curse."

"And you could break it." The Goblin Queen lunged forward again, brushed her claws down either side of Freya's face. "You beat him once, Freya. All you have to do is break the curse. Take my place, and then he will breathe again. I'll let him go. He'll live again and you will be the one who saved him. I promise, I won't let him forget that."

Something was missing from this explanation. Something horrible and evil because that was who the Goblin Queen was in her core.

"You said I would be able to see him breathing," Freya quietly said. "That's how you started this whole deal. Was that the truth?"

The Goblin Queen's gaze shifted into darkness. "No, my dear. You won't see him alive again. This story will end in tragedy, I'm afraid. But you will know that you gave up your life so that he could live. And if anyone could beat me, it would be him. So wouldn't it be smarter for you to make sure Eldridge has that chance?"

But Freya could beat her. She had beaten Eldridge at his own game, so couldn't she do the same for this woman?

Those claws scraped down her cheeks. Tiny pinpricks of cold trailed from her eyes as though she were crying frozen tears.

The Goblin Queen hissed. "No, don't think like that, Freya. You're only going to disappoint yourself. You cannot beat me, and you wouldn't ever have the chance again. If you don't agree to this deal, then I will simply take matters into my own hands. You will join the goblin man you think you have fallen in love with, and everything will end now."

Well, she didn't have an option then, did she?

Freya took a deep breath and then let it out with all the tension in her body. "I will take his place then, Goblin Queen."

CHAPTER 26

The moment she agreed, the frozen faerie's arms moved. He released her with a creaking sound, like an iron gate opening. Freya stepped out of the frigid grip and shook herself.

A fine coating of snow already laid on top of her starry cloak. The fabric was ripped at the edges, too light now to give her any amount of heat. The ice had taken its toll on Eldridge's magic. As it would for all time, she supposed.

"Follow me," the Goblin Queen said. She lifted a hand over her head and then strode away as though she didn't worry that Freya would come along behind her. Freya was merely a pawn in this game.

And that was the root of the problem, wasn't it?

The madness of the ball, the sudden and swift change that happened in the matter of seconds had shocked them all. Eldridge had been so prepared to destroy the Goblin Queen with one nimble blow. But they hadn't worked together on this at all. He had run the entire battle without telling his soldier where to go.

Meanwhile, the Goblin Queen simply controlled all her

pieces on the board with finesse and grace. She had created a mindless army that did her bidding without question. That plan still had its flaws, though. Freya knew those weaknesses were equally dangerous.

Soldiers who could think and feel were the only ones to see situations from another angle. The Goblin Queen was relying on herself and herself alone.

That was an opportunity.

She just had to figure out how that was an opportunity before the Queen froze her solid.

Taking the Queen's place in Eldridge's curse was a risk she was willing to take. Freya could only stall for so long, but she needed time right now. Time to think. To plan. To live, if that's what it came down to.

Freya reached into her pocket and touched a hand to the knife that was still wrapped up in fabric. The sharp edges were wearing away at their covering, and she knew it was a sign. She had to use the knife. She had to at least try to finish this game, even if that meant fighting to the bitter end.

Otherwise, she would die. She didn't trust that the Goblin Queen would let Eldridge go, either. Right now was the moment Eldridge had spoken of.

The Goblin Queen thought she had won. All of that confidence was running through her veins, telling her that no one could beat her now. She could let her guard down. The ball simply hadn't been the right moment to strike.

Freya followed the Queen through the blue ice halls. Head held high and jaw set as though she knew she was going to her grave. It was easy to pretend, because she very well could be seeing her last visions of the place.

As they strode through the halls, swiftly moving over the ice, Freya only had one regret.

She wished she had apologized to Arrow better. She wished they had talked about the awkwardness between them, and that she had the time to mend their relationship before she had to take this risk. After all, the goblin had become a very dear friend to her.

Even if he was a goblin. Perhaps that was the strangest change in her life. Not the Goblin King. Not losing her sister. But becoming friends with one of the creatures she had once hated. Close friends that she could only hope would get a chance to know each other better.

The Goblin Queen opened a door at the very end of the castle and gestured for Freya to step out into the storm. "Walk, mortal. This is your last chance to see the beauty in the world. So I suggest you look your fill."

At the end of her words, the storm stopped. Snowflakes fell gently through the air, settling in a fine layer of untouched diamond dust. A light wind blew through the flakes, ruffling the snow mounds and revealing a frozen lake of the purest blue. The sky overhead mimicked the color until the whole world was painted white and azure. The air was filled with a heady silence. Like it was waiting to be filled with song.

This was hidden behind the storm? All this natural beauty that filled the heart with a longing for something unnamed.

Freya knew she was staring. That her eyes were ridiculously wide and that maybe her jaw had fallen open. But she hadn't realized the castle was surrounded by so much elegance. So much possibility for it to be a lovely place that artists flocked to for inspiration. Why would she want to hide all this with a storm?

The Goblin Queen paused beside her. A faint wind stirred her curls that had fallen out of their tight braid. "Lovely. Isn't it?"

"Yes." Freya furrowed her brows and clenched her hand in the fabric of her dress. "Why are you letting me see this now?"

"I'm not a heartless wretch," the Goblin Queen replied. "I know he wanted you to think that my heart is frozen, but I know the sacrifice you're going to make. I understand that you must feel afraid of death, even though I will never experience that myself. No one should go through that fear by herself."

A moment of kindness from a woman she had been led to believe didn't know how to feel that emotion at all. Freya wished she could convince the Goblin Queen to change. To give them all a chance to figure this out together. But she knew as well as the other woman that there was no stopping what either of them had to do.

The battle of wits had only just begun.

They walked across the ice together. Quietly admiring the sunlight dancing on the mirror-like surface and the frozen bubbles rising beneath their feet. The ice was crystal clear and perfectly flat. Though no fish swam in the depths, Freya had a feeling they would come alive if only a little heat were allowed to enter this place.

Finally, they reached the end of the lake where a great, twisting sculpture of ice created large gates. They stood open, waiting for anyone who wanted to enter with open arms.

"What is this place?" she asked.

"It's the royal burial grounds." The Goblin Queen stepped through the gates, her gown swishing around her legs. "This is where I laid my mother and father to rest. It's where most of the Winter Court waits for the curse to be broken. And it will be where you remain for all time."

Buried. She was going to be buried alive?

Freya's stomach twisted in fear. She walked hesitantly after the Goblin Queen, now understanding just how grave any misstep would be.

The burial grounds were exquisite, just like the rest of the Winter Court. Her fears dimmed as she saw the many altars instead of graves. The winter faeries didn't put their bodies in the solid ground, apparently, although that made sense considering how difficult it would be to dig up the frozen earth.

Instead, each person was encased in an ice coffin. Like tiny little greenhouses placed all around the grounds. Each coffin was unique in its own way. Some of the patchwork patterns of silver framing resembled snowflakes. Others had created a warm biome inside the ice, flowers growing through their finger and vines wrapping around their wrists in loving embraces.

Freya would rather be warm in death, she supposed. Though it wasn't really death, was it? She was expected to take on a curse. Alive, but not awake. An eternity like that would seem as if she would live in a dreaming world. Would she even be able to hear someone talking to her?

"Here we are," the Goblin Queen said. Her words sliced through Freya's nightmarish thoughts.

In the very center of the burial grounds was a large stone altar. A large ice cover protected the woman within, although this one was made of pristine, clear ice. Freya was horrified to realize someone was already laid to rest upon the altar.

The woman was unnaturally beautiful, with long dark locks that reached her waist in fluffy curls. Her blue gown spilled around her hips and draped over the grey stone. Whoever had buried her, had folded her hands gracefully on her chest. Long dark lashes fanned out over her curved cheeks.

"Who was she?" Freya asked.

She stepped up to the altar and looked down at the hands delicately folded over the woman's heart. Tiny half moons of blue decorated her nails.

"Someone who everyone thought was so lovely that the sun wouldn't set on her face." The Goblin Queen snorted. "Obviously the sun sets on anything and everyone. And though she is still pretty in death, I highly doubt anyone wants her now."

The Goblin Queen planted her hands on the ice top and gave it a quick shove. The arced ice slid too easily, slipping off the altar and hitting the ground. It shattered like too thin glass. Shards spilled over the ground beyond the altar, skittering every which way.

Freya almost expected the woman to open her eyes in fear. The sound was loud enough to wake the dead, and yet, the woman remained still and silent.

The Goblin Queen then put her hands on the corpse and shoved. The body slid from the altar onto the ground with a wet thump that had Freya turning her face away from the desecration. Sweat slicked her palms, and she squeezed her eyes shut in hopes that this would all go away.

Who was so cruel that they would remove the dead from their final resting place?

"So much better." The Goblin Queen dusted her hands off on her dress and grinned. "I think this place would be more fitting for you than that little witch."

"Obviously you did not like the woman," Freya observed. She took a deep breath to still her nerves, then forced herself to look back at the Queen.

"No. But I do like you, Freya. I want to put you in a place of honor so that when the time comes, we can all look at the woman who broke Eldridge's curse. We'll make sure to put flowers on your coffin, I promise you that." The Goblin Queen lifted her hands and blue magic spilled from her fingertips in a sparkling rain shower. "I'll make yours the most splendid one in my garden."

Garden? Was this what the Goblin Queen called her garden?

Freya reminded herself that she still had to play the game. She couldn't sit around waiting for the Goblin Queen to make a misstep. She had to take control over this situation or everything would fall apart. Just like she was afraid it would.

So she played the game.

Freya clambered up onto the altar and sat down with a hard thump. The stone was ice cold. The backs of her legs ached, and she wished for more layers in her skirts. Compared to the woman who had laid here before, Freya felt small and insignificant. Her feet weren't even close to the end.

Patting the stone around her, she arranged her legs as the previous woman had them. "Now what?" she asked.

"Now you are going to take the curse from me." The Goblin

Queen frowned. "I thought you knew that? Lay down, Freya. I'll transfer it to you and then everything will simply go dark for you. It will be painless, my dear."

Why did all the faeries keep saying that to her? None of this was painless. For any of them.

She tried to hide her shaking hands in the folds of her dress as she laid down on the cold stone. She could feel the pinpricks of ice digging into her back. The sky spread out above her, not a cloud in sight. And yes, it was a beautiful day to die.

But she had no intent on dying.

Blue tendrils of magic spread from the ground. They slithered over her body, stretching over her arms and hands, holding her down onto the altar. Like thick icicles, they forced her to remain still as the Goblin Queen began her chant.

Freya could feel the curse. Strangely, it was familiar. Eldridge's magic had been around her for such a long time, it would be hard not to recognize the feeling. It moved through her body, solidifying her legs first. And what a horrible thing to attack. It meant she couldn't run if she wanted to. That claustrophobic feeling might drive a person mad long before the curse put them to sleep.

And though she wanted to put her plan into action now, she waited. Because she wasn't the kind of person to rush headlong into battle. She would take her time. She would wait until the moment was right.

The ice stretched up to her hips, then her chest. Her heart stuttered in the cold grip of magic. It wanted to keep beating, but the ice wanted it to stop.

As the magic reached her neck, Freya croaked out a simple, "Wait."

She hoped the Goblin Queen suffered from the same flaw as every faerie she had met thus far. The flaw that meant they all were so easily controlled, even though they didn't realize that was what happened.

Curiosity.

The Goblin Queen fell into her trap with almost no complaint. The magic stuttered, hesitated, and then held her frozen in place.

Lumi, the Winter Princess, and now Goblin Queen, leaned over Freya's prone body. Her beautiful face was silhouetted by the vivid blue sky. "What is it? Last words are an honorable thing, I suppose. But if you could hurry up, that would make this all easier."

Freya purposefully kept her voice too quiet to hear. She whispered nonsense that no one would have been able to understand. Because the words didn't matter, she just needed Lumi to get closer.

"What?" The Goblin Queen leaned down until her ear almost pressed to Freya's lips.

It was all the opportunity Freya needed. She had remembered what her mother always claimed, and the teaching that would actually save her daughter.

Magic came down to one thing. Belief.

And in that moment, she let Arrow's words fly through her soul. She let his belief consume her and fill her heart.

She had magic. She was more than just a mortal and she could break this Goblin Queen's power if she wanted to. And so she did.

Her arm shifted, wiggled beneath the grip of ice and cold. Freya wrapped her fingers around the hilt of the icy blade and gripped it tight.

"Your greatest flaw has always been your pride," she whispered into the Goblin Queen's ear.

And then she lifted the blade between them and plunged it deep into Lumi's heart.

A sound echoed through the graveyard like a great boom of an ancient beast screaming. The Goblin Queen arched away from her, a gasp echoing through her lips that turned into a painful wheeze. Cold blood dripped down the hilt of the knife. Freya's hands turned slick with it.

The Goblin Queen pressed her hands against her chest where the hilt of the blade had stuck. She braced herself with one arm over Freya. This time, it was Lumi's eyes that were held wide with shock.

The strength of the Goblin Queen's magic faded. Freya's body warmed, though it was still too chilly for comfort. And there were more important things here than her own comfort.

She shifted, holding onto Lumi and helping her ease down onto the altar. The once Goblin Queen gasped in a few breaths, though they were stuttering and slow. Each pant seemed to come at a great price as dark blood spread from her back.

Freya stared down at the woman who was so certain she had won. Her heart filled with pity.

She couldn't leave this woman to die alone.

So she sat beside her and held Lumi's hand. With soft touches, she stroked the palm that had once controlled so much magic.

Freya sighed. "Unlike you, I am actually kind. You were right, you know. No one should have to face the fear of death alone. I think you would have left me alone, and you would have liked knowing I was afraid. I won't do that to you."

Lumi's hand flexed. Her fingers clawed at Freya's, desperately trying to hold on to the mortal woman. "I don't want to die."

"No one does." Tears slipped down Freya's cheeks, warm and likely undeserved for this woman who had done so much harm. "But you won't face it alone. I promise."

Freya stayed. She didn't know how long it took for this evil woman to slip away. But even in the darkest moments of Lumi's life, she was still that heartbroken little girl. Weakened by magic and pain.

She waited with her enemy until the last rattling breath filled the burial grounds.

The Winter Princess lost her grip on the mortal hero's hand.

The delicate fingers slipped down onto the altar where they would remain for all eternity. Limp. Powerless. And finally at rest.

Freya leaned forward, held her head in her hands, and sobbed.

CHAPTER 27

reya had no idea how long she sat in those burial grounds. It might have been a few moments, it might have been hours.

She had killed a person. Even though the Goblin Queen had been evil and horrible, she still had a right to live. Or at least, that's what it felt like now that Freya had murdered the woman.

Eventually, her tears dried up, and she knew she had to go. People needed her. She couldn't remain here feeling sorry for herself. Even though killing someone for the first time did feel appropriate to languish in agony.

The blood had dried on her hands, but it still soaked her dress. The Goblin Queen's magic had changed the fabric of her gown where her life force lingered. It was a pale bluish lavender now. Completely lacking in the vibrant colors the Goblin King had given her.

The hem was soaked in blood. Her hands were covered in it, and a splatter had stained the side of her dress. She was quite literally marked as a killer. Anyone who saw her would know what she had done.

Would she ever get better at this? The wound she had inflicted on the Goblin Queen seemed to spread through her own body until she couldn't quite tell whether she had harmed herself or not.

Perhaps the smartest thing to do would be to get out of this place where dead people rested.

She stood, stumbling off the altar and making her way to the entrance. The frozen lake spread out before her and the storm hadn't started up again. Was that all the Goblin Queen? The blizzard might have been a symbol of the Queen's internal struggle. Or... Something. A cry for help? A wish she'd made as a child gone wrong?

Freya's mind wasn't working right. Belatedly, she realized that was an issue she would have to figure out. Her heart wasn't in it anymore. She wanted to go home. She wanted to break down and cry, or maybe just fall over and let all of this end here. After all she'd done, she was so damned tired.

Freya shambled over the ice like one of the dead had risen out of the cemetery. Each step was a shuffle of sorts. Picking up her feet was harder than it had been before she had this massive amount of guilt on her shoulders. She could feel that guilt weighing her down, dragging behind her with every movement.

"Freya?" Eldridge's voice called out over the ice.

The frozen lake groaned beneath her, almost as though it didn't want the Goblin King to find the woman who had killed Lumi. Or maybe she was the one who had groaned.

She knew what she must look like. Blood stained gown billowing in the slight breeze. A knife clutched in her hand, but one she didn't remember removing from the Goblin Queen's heart. When had she pulled that out? Or had she ever really let it go?

She stared down at the blue blade and could remember the popping feeling of flesh. It had slid in between the Goblin Queen's ribs so easily. Like she had been born to kill someone. As if it was easy, when it should have been very difficult.

"Freya," Eldridge called out to her again.

She wanted to turn away from him and run. He shouldn't see her like this.

No one should see someone after they had so easily taken a life.

Eldridge slammed into her like she'd hit a wall. He tugged her hard against his chest, catching the hand that held the blade and holding it away from the two of them. They must have looked like they were dancing.

"My hero," he whispered into her hair. "You're covered in blood, Freya. Where are you hurt?"

"I'm not." She pressed the words numbly into his shoulder. Her lips stiff with cold. "I'm not hurt at all."

"Who's blood is this, then?" He sank onto his knees, drawing her down into his lap on the cold ice. "Freya, you're frightening me. Please, tell me what happened. Let go of the knife, darling."

She tried. She really did. Freya wiggled her fingers, but the cold knife was stuck to her fingers. Fused, as if it didn't want to let go of her.

Eldridge leaned back and helped pry it free from her grip. Painstakingly, he opened each and every one of her fingers, drawing them open and shaking the knife off of her skin.

The blade hit the ice with a solid thunk. Then, the lake split like the mouth of a fish opening up. Bubbles from deep beneath them caused the fissure, traveling through the ice until they reached the knife. They devoured the magical object, drawing it deep into the darkness until she couldn't see it anymore.

At least the Winter Court had taken back the only weapon that could destroy the person who would lead it. Freya didn't want the responsibility anymore.

Eldridge cupped her face, forcing her gaze to return to his. "Are you hurt?"

"No." Not physically. She wasn't sure yet what was going on in her head. She had a sick feeling in her stomach that this memory would come up again for a very long time.

Lumi's eyes hadn't been that magical blue when she died.

They had faded into an almost silver. Metallic, dull, and lacking of any emotion.

Had she been afraid when she died?

His thumbs smoothed over her cheekbones, eyes searching hers to see if she was telling him the truth. "What happened?"

"It's over." She couldn't tell him everything that she'd done. She couldn't. Freya stared at her bloody hand resting on his shoulder. "The Goblin Queen is gone."

"Yes, I knew that. I woke up and I can feel all my powers are back, as well as the responsibility of my throne." He squeezed her jaw ever so slightly, forcing her to focus on him. "You don't seem like yourself, dear one. Not at all."

She didn't feel like herself.

Wiggling free from his grip, Freya tucked herself underneath Eldridge's chin and tried very hard not to start crying again. "I didn't want to do it," she whispered. "She didn't deserve to die, but I didn't... There wasn't another way."

"I know." Eldridge tightened his arms around her. "I know you did all you could to convince her otherwise. She wouldn't have changed for anyone, Freya."

"But she did." Her voice was thick with emotion. Memories from just an hour before burned behind her closed eyes. "She wanted me to see the sky before I died. The storm disappeared long before we reached the burial grounds. Lumi still wanted me to see something beautiful before I saw nothing at all. Surely that meant she was still capable of some kindness."

"No, Freya. It means she saw the value of beauty, that's all." He splayed his hands across her back, rubbing gently. Easing the torment of her soul. "I will remind you a thousand times over if you need me to, but you did the right thing. My dear. My wonderful hero of this story and every tale that you are drawn into. You saved us all."

But why did it feel like she had saved no one? Or she supposed that she had saved everyone at the cost of someone who maybe hadn't deserved what she got?

She shook in his arms. No matter how embarrassed she was about her reaction, she couldn't stop shivering. And she wasn't cold. She didn't feel the frigid air or the ice beneath them.

Eldridge's arms flexed, and a blast of warm air surrounded them. "I think I am the one who needs to help you, now."

"How so?"

"You're missing pieces of yourself. It happens when you..." He drew back and cupped her face again. He threaded his fingers through her hair, gently scraping his nails over her scalp. "We won't talk about it for a while. But when you're ready, I'll help you. I promise."

Though it didn't make her feel a world of difference, at least she knew he would be there for her. And when she found the pieces she had lost... Freya hoped that he would give her the smallest bit of kindness and handle them with care.

Footsteps echoed over the ice. First, the sound of heels, then clicking claws, then a thunderous sound like a hundred feet all approaching at once. An army?

Freya lifted her head from Eldridge's shoulder and watched with shock as what appeared to be the entire Winter Court walked over the frozen lake. Many of them she recognized from the dance. But some were new faces she'd never seen.

Arrow and Frost led them toward the couple who were curled into each other. Both her new companions' faces were filled with shock and hope that this was all over. That after every moment of fighting and scheming, that their true King had returned.

She didn't want them to see her like this. Pressing her face back to his warm neck, she blew out a long sigh. "I'm covered in blood. They're going to think me mad."

"No, they're going to think you've saved them all." He tilted his head and kissed the side of her face. His lips burned, and she wondered just how cold she was. "But if you'd prefer not to show any signs of your battle, then I suppose I can help with that."

Magic warmed her from the toes up. All the blood washed

off her body like she had taken a shower and she felt her dress rip at the hem. It dissolved at her feet, the gown now knee length and still as lovely as ever.

The magic made her feel fresh and clean. Not like she had just killed a woman, but that she was taken care of.

The transformation did remind her, however, that she wasn't the same person as she had been walking into that graveyard with the faerie she'd left behind.

She was a new woman now. Not a faerie, not a mortal, but something in between.

Eldridge helped her stand up and face the crowd of people. He held her hand in his, connected and united. No matter what the Winter Court thought of them after they had killed the Princess.

"My King!" Arrow called. The grin on his face was infectious. Even Frost looked like he was smiling underneath that strange icy cage of a head. "We're glad to see the rightful king take back his throne."

"Not quite yet, my friend. I still have to return to the Goblin castle and piece it back together." Eldridge squeezed her fingers. "There's still a lot of work to be done."

She couldn't help but feel like he was talking about her, as well. And there was a lot of work for her to do. Yet again, she felt like she was floating and there was no one there to catch her when she fell off the edge of the waterfall in her mind. Sure, she was holding onto Eldridge like he was the only lifeline she had. But what if he didn't want to be that person for her?

Her breathing was too ragged. She was going to lose it in front of all of these people. They wouldn't understand what was happening to her. How could they?

Faeries killed each other all the time. They waged wars, and they dealt with the emotions that came from them. If they even felt guilt at all. But she had never killed anyone before today, and that weight pressed against her shoulders. It held her down into the ice like the Goblin Queen herself was still holding onto her shoulders. Whispering that she had become a monster while trying to be a hero.

Arrow padded closer, his brows drawn down in a frown. Wringing his tiny paws, he stared at her with hope in his eyes. "Freya? Might I be of assistance?"

She released her hold on Eldridge's hand and dropped to her knees. Dragging the goblin dog into her arms felt like she was finally hugging a friend. Someone who could see her fall apart without judgement, because he was and always would be there for her.

"Arrow," she whispered into his furry neck. "I'm so sorry for everything that happened. I didn't know how to… I still don't…"

He rested his head on her shoulder and let out a long, happy sigh. "I forgive you, Miss Freya. I will always forgive you. No matter what."

At least some weight lifted from her shoulders.

Someone cleared their throat and stepped out of the crowd of icy faeries. He was taller than the others, with broad shoulders that tapered into a trim waist. He held his hands at his sides, open and inviting. "My King. Please allow me to be the very first to welcome you back."

Eldridge looked the man over with a light in his eyes that she knew was a little too calculating. "So you'll be the one who takes over for her, is that it?"

This man would be the new Winter Prince?

Freya looked him over and tried to see through the thin veil of his power. She wanted to know if he would be a good man. Or in the very least, if he would take care of the court she and Eldridge were leaving behind.

Shockingly, she could suddenly see his future. Glimpses of what he would be, or could be, if he let himself.

He wouldn't be the kindest of leaders. He would fall in with the other court rulers very well, though. His heart wasn't pure, and his intentions weren't just, but he would lead the kingdom well. They would understand his desires. They would agree to do what he ordered.

Order was a good word for him. He liked things neat. Tidy. Exactly where he placed them.

When Freya looked up at Eldridge, he had stiffened in shock. His hands flexed at his side, but he wasn't looking at the other faerie. He was looking at her.

"What?" she asked.

He swallowed, Adam's apple bobbing up and down. "What do you think of him, Freya?"

"I think he'll suit the court just fine." She tightened her grip on Arrow for a brief moment before releasing him. "And I think for once, I'd like to not worry about the Winter Court for a little while. Don't you agree?"

Eldridge was still too stiff. He nodded curtly and then replied to the faerie man, "You'll do. Take the throne and do your people proud. Be a better leader than the one who fell, would you?"

The faerie bowed, low and deep. His dark hair nearly touched the ice, melding in with the color. Freya lost control of her balance. She couldn't tell where the ice was and where the faerie man's hair started. When she looked at the other faeries to try and distract herself, all their dresses seemed to meld into the frigid surface as well. There was no longer an up or a down. Just a constantly moving ice that threatened to swallow her whole.

She might have laid down to still her stomach, but someone else interrupted her thoughts.

Pale hands streaked with dark smudges snapped their fingers in front of her face.

Jerking back, she stared up in shock at eyes that were very familiar. Black eyes that had caused more trouble than they were worth.

"You?" she whispered.

The birch faerie grinned down at her. And sure, he wasn't exactly put together right. In fact, she would argue that the cracks along his face made him look like a mosaic. Just as she had feared.

But he was alive. Well. And apparently healthy, considering he hopped away at Eldridge's angry growl.

"I wanted to say thank you," the birch faerie said. "You helped my friend put me back together, and I know I wouldn't be where I am today without your intervention. That means a lot, Miss Freya. And I don't usually say such pleasant words."

No, she suspected that he didn't.

Releasing her tight grip on Arrow, she shakily stood. "Well, it's the least I could do for taking your Queen."

The faerie's cheeks turned bright red. He looked over his shoulder at the big faerie who had remained in the crowd. "We never much liked her anyway, miss. She always made things a little too... difficult. We had to focus on staying alive. Play to her whims. When really we just wanted to focus on each other."

Oh.

And there was one of those pieces she had been missing, like Eldridge said. It fit right into her soul where she remembered how important it was to save people like this. People who had forgotten how to love, but could now do so freely.

Tears in her eyes, she pressed her side against Eldridge's. "Can we go home now?" she asked.

"The mortal realm won't look kindly on you or your sister," he replied. "Are you sure you want to take that risk?"

She hadn't even realized she'd said the wrong word. Or perhaps the wrong term for what she thought of as home now.

Freya looked up into his starry night eyes, and said, "I want to go home with you, Eldridge. I want to see my sister and help put the kingdom to rights. I don't want to go back to my cabin in the woods."

His eyes widened. "Oh."

"Yes. Oh." She smiled, though the expression felt fragile now.

Eldridge wrapped an arm around her waist and pulled her beneath his arm. "Yes, Freya. We can go home now."

CHAPTER 28

Though strange, returning to the Goblin Court did very much feel like returning home. Freya hadn't realized how close Eldridge lived to the other courts. It felt as though that starry kingdom was so far removed from the others, that he could never have seen them.

And yet, his castle was right around the corner from the Autumn Court. But then again, when she thought about it, that made a lot of sense.

He would want to be close to his home. Why wouldn't he? Though he'd left the Autumn Court for a while, they were still where his roots had grown.

Arrow stopped with them just before the castle, then bowed low. His suit was looking a little ragged, but he still somehow appeared quite noble as he bowed. "My King, as always, it is an honor to save the kingdom with you."

"And you, my friend." Eldridge looked on, amused, as Arrow stepped up to Freya's side.

"Miss Freya." He wrung his paws, looking first at the ground, then up at her. "I hope you will come and visit a lonely old goblin in his meager home someday."

She tapped a finger against her chin, taking her time to ponder the question. "Will you have tea?" she asked.

"I suppose if you want tea, then yes I could have some ready for you."

"Arrow, I don't know how to tell you this, but your tea is quite horrid." She tried very hard to suppress the smile on her lips, but couldn't quite contain it. "I'd prefer it greatly if you didn't serve me tea any longer. Then I'd be happy to come to your home. Quite happy indeed."

And just like that, it was as if she had never said those things all those months ago. It didn't matter that she had been careless. Nor did it matter that she had tried to end their friendship when it had just begun.

Freya and Arrow's relationship was fine again. And for that, she was very grateful.

Arrow dropped back onto all fours and left. He was likely returning to his home, hoping that her sister and Lux hadn't destroyed the place. She could only hope that they hadn't, although Esther wasn't particularly neat.

She had a feeling they would all know if Esther hadn't treated the goblin dog's home with respect.

With a soft smile on her face, she returned her attention to the Goblin King. He stood in the center of a small field, his castle silhouetted behind him. The spires twisted with stairs on their exterior, beautiful and unreal. Stars could just barely be seen glittering in the sky around the castle, although the sun was still on the horizon. She didn't know how it looked like a galaxy flared to life behind the building, but it certainly did.

He reached out his hand. "You said you wanted to come home."

She did. More than anything. Freya took his hand without hesitation and let him draw her toward the very sky where he had made his kingdom. "Where do you think my sister and Lux are?"

"If I know the friends of the Goblin King, then I think your sister and Lux will be waiting for us in the castle." He wrapped his arm around her shoulders and drew her close. "Now, the story I'm going to tell everyone will be quite tragic. I want them to pity me, you see. It's been a long time since I've been in such trouble that someone has had to save me."

"Ah." Freya nodded. "Of course. You will want their sympathy, that makes sense. How can I assist in this elaborate lie?"

"It's not a lie." He pressed a hand against his chest dramatically. "I would never lie to anyone. I'm a faerie. This is merely the same story that we just lived. Elaborated, perhaps, but only for dramatic effect."

"Isn't that a lie?"

"Of course not." He winked. "It's the gift of a storyteller and every bit my right as the person who suffered so greatly to defeat the Goblin Queen."

They strode through the front gates of his castle, and she shook her head. "Absolutely not. I was the one who defeated the Goblin Queen. You can't take that title away from me. I am now the only person to defeat not one, but two people who hold your very station."

He stuck out his tongue. "I suppose you're right. It is unbefitting of a gentleman to steal a lady's title without asking."

"Truer words have never been said."

Eldridge remained silent for a few moments. He waltzed them all the way to the front door before clearing his throat and asking, "Then I suppose it does no harm to ask if I might steal your title. Just for dramatic effect."

Freya laughed, looking up at him with all the mirth she could muster contained in her chest. "Thank you very much for asking, Goblin King. But no. I would like the title for as long as I might keep it."

He sighed, then draped himself over her shoulder. She stumbled with the sudden weight that was hanging off her. Like he was some war battered man who needed her to help keep him upright. "Then you will tell them I was gravely injured, which I was mind you, and that I needed to be carried back to my throne. Then, when I sit on it, we will reveal that I have been healed by the power of the Goblin King, and everyone will be left in awe."

The laughter that burst out of her was filled with a sense of relief. He was back to his normal self, finally. Ridiculous and quite possibly the strangest man she had ever met. But he was back to being her Goblin King. "I will do no such thing. But I can help you into the castle if you need a woman to drag you."

"Would that make me look weak?"

She stared into those swirling silver eyes and shook her head. "I don't think you could ever look weak, Goblin King. You took the throne back, even if you had the help of a mortal woman."

His joking expression softened. Eldridge tucked a strand of her hair behind her ear and quietly said, "Or perhaps not so much of a mortal as we thought. You used magic on the ice, Freya. I think that shouldn't just be swept under the carpet so quickly."

"Perhaps not. But let's get settled into this new life first, shall we?"

Together, they opened the doors and strode into the room where she had first met the Goblin King. The golden planets weaved overhead, although they weren't so dangerously close as to hit them now.

Three figures stood in the very center of the room. Two with tails, and one with horns that just missed clipping a passing planet.

"Freya!" Esther shouted, running to her sister and throwing herself into Freya's arms. "You made it! I can't believe it, but you actually did it!"

Lux grinned behind Esther and added, "Again. You did it again."

"Did you ever doubt me?" Freya peeled herself out of Esther's arms and tried very hard to look at least a little disappointed. "I beat the Goblin Queen, yes. But it wasn't easy."

"Beating the leader of a court is rarely easy." The deep, smooth voice was one that Freya had hoped to hear again in her lifetime.

The Autumn Thief strode toward them with her hands tucked behind her back. There was the slightest bit of fur on her antlers, and Freya feared that meant they would shed soon. She quite liked the antlers on the redhead. This time, the Thief wore a lovely corseted dress in a deep, vibrant green. The bodice was tight to her flat chest, and the corset created a lovely hourglass figure tucked in tight at her hips.

"Autumn Thief," Freya said with a grin. "It's good to see you again so soon."

"With information you'll be pleased to hear this time." The Autumn Thief extended her arm. "Would you follow me, please? I've been waiting quite a long time to speak with you."

Freya frowned. She looked at Eldridge, hoping he would have some kind of reaction. But he appeared just as confused as she was.

They had only walked in the doors a moment ago. What else could she need to hear that was so important?

Esther nudged her toward the Thief. "Go on, Freya. I'll fill in the Goblin King. But I think you need to hear this from the Autumn Thief yourself."

Did her sister know what the Autumn Thief was going to say? That made everything even more suspicious. Freya didn't have the emotional capacity to handle returning to the court, let alone whatever else had gone wrong.

But she would go forward and do whatever the Autumn Thief wanted. Because of all the court leaders, this was the only one she thought had Freya's best interests at heart.

She followed the Autumn Thief past a few of the planets to an alcove she hadn't seen before. The space was filled with tiny silver stars hanging from the ceiling and softly dancing in a breeze she couldn't feel. A metal bench had been poured to look like it was the tail of a comet that burst out of one side, glowing with a faint white light.

Freya sat down, pinned her shaking hands to her lap, and cleared her throat. "All right, then. What is it now?"

"Not just yet. I want to make sure you're all right, first." The Autumn Thief sat down next to her and gathered Freya's hands in her own. "You just went through a great struggle. I can feel that much. I don't want you to fall apart at the seams, Freya. Your place here is still very uncertain, but I believe you to be capable of far greater things than you've even accomplished thus far."

Freya nearly broke down again. She wanted to let the words tumble from her tongue that she wasn't all right. Maybe she never would be again. She was still haunted by the image of the Winter Princess dying. The knowledge that she had taken a life, and that she hadn't really fought all that hard to not take it.

But she couldn't blame anyone other than herself. The knife had been in her hand. She had made the decision to plunge it into the Winter Princess's breast and it had been far, far too easy.

The Autumn Thief squeezed Freya's fingers, bringing her back into the present. "Dealing with death is never easy. I'm afraid I cannot help you with that. But perhaps I might address an underlying issue that is causing your inability to focus on anything but what you had to do in that frozen place?"

Nothing else was bothering Freya. She couldn't focus on anything other than what she'd done.

Frowning, she stared into the Autumn Thief's eyes that slowly changed from a deep brown to a vivid green. "I don't know what you're talking about. I can't think of anything else but her."

"You won't let yourself think of anything else. Because if you had a few moments of rest in your mind, you would realize you fear that you no longer have a purpose. There is no more evil villain for you to defeat. No more reason for you to be a hero."

The Thief tilted her head to the side. "Look inside yourself, Freya. Do you really fear the memory of death? Or the sudden existence of a threat you cannot fight?"

She swallowed hard. "I will make a place for myself here, in this court."

"No, you won't. You're so certain that no one could ever need you here, that you will continue to apply yourself to this one, singular memory." The Thief smiled softly. She released her grip on Freya and smoothed a hand down her corset. "But I am here to give you a new purpose. Ever since you were in my court, I knew there was something different about you. About your sister. There were too many questions left unanswered. So I did some digging."

Freya pressed a hand to her aching temples. This time, not from Eldridge's magic, but from the pounding of too much pressure. "I don't think I can take another person musing that I'm not human. I've already heard it from enough people today."

"That's not what the Autumn Thief is trying to tell you," Eldridge said.

She startled at the sound of his voice. Freya pressed her hand to her thundering heart and wheezed out a long breath. "Don't sneak up on me like that, Eldridge."

"Sorry." He put both his hands on her shoulders, squeezing tightly like he was here to give her support. "Go ahead and tell her, Thief."

Oh no.

What were they going to say?

Worry spearing through her chest, she waited for someone else to hit her over the head. What could be worse than the Autumn Thief knowing what kind of faerie she was? Or had come from?

The Thief cleared her throat. "I know where your mother is, Freya. She's alive and I believe she's currently being held in the Spring Court."

A scream built in Freya's chest, but she refused to let it out. Instead, she whispered, "My mother?"

"Yes, my dear. She's here in the faerie realms."

Eldridge held tight to her shoulders as she started to shake. Freya didn't know what to do with this information. Her mother was dead. She had been dead for many years. Missing, of course. But eventually a person had to give up looking and realize that the loved one who had run away was no longer alive.

Except she'd been wrong.

Eldridge sat down beside her on the bench, pulled her against his side, and pressed his lips to her head. "We'll find her, Freya. I promise you."

So many promises.

She put her head to his heart and for the first time in her life, prayed to the old gods and the new. Her prayer was a simple one.

Please, let the Goblin King keep his promise.

The Story Continues in Of Pixies and Spells - Coming May 15th!

Preorder today!

ABOUT THE AUTHOR

Emma Hamm is a small town girl on a blueberry field in Maine. She writes stories that remind her of home, of fairytales, and of myths and legends that make her mind wander.

She can be found by the fireplace with a cup of tea and her two Maine Coon cats dipping their paws into the water without her knowing.

Subscribe to my Newsletter for updates on new stories!
www.emmahamm.com

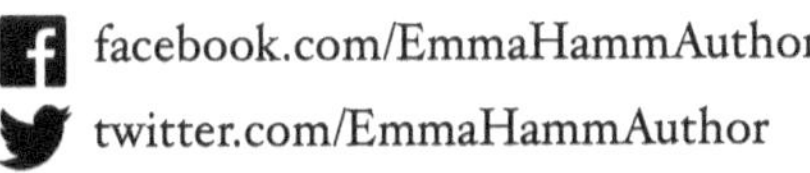

facebook.com/EmmaHammAuthor
twitter.com/EmmaHammAuthor
instagram.com/emmahammauthor